Amish Amity

Natalie Moore

Published by Trellis Publishing, 2021.

This is a work of fiction. Similarities to real people, places, or events are entirely coincidental.

AMISH AMITY

First edition. July 15, 2021.

Copyright © 2021 Natalie Moore.

ISBN: 979-8224956487

Written by Natalie Moore.

AMISH AMITY

Marisa Meyer

AMISH AMITY

Three best friends, Betty, Amity and Rachel are practically inseparable. But when they land themselves in a stormy predicament on their way home on night a newcomer in town comes to their rescue. All three girls show an interest in the handsome stranger, but only one of them would walk away with the prize. What starts off as nothing but a playful bet between friends, ends up surprising them all.

Uri Guth came to Derby Creek to start afresh, the last thing he expected was to fall in love. But when he meets the shy red head who reminded him autumn, he pulled out all stops. He knew the moment he laid eyes on her that she was his match.

Chapter 1

Rain just kept falling, never ending without any intention to stop, large puddles had gathered on the muddy grounds around the big barn, and water gushed down the eroded embankment running alongside the road, causing the road to be completely flooded. But no amount of rain would prevent Amity, Betty and Rachel to do what they came here to do. Having been friends since childhood, the three women were inseparable. Neither of them were married or promised to anyone yet, and although they are well beyond the age most girls in their community starts to settle down to start a family, it never really bothered them.

Amity was strong willed and mouthy young woman, who voiced her opinion whenever she felt it mattered. Of course her father, Bishop Gunther didn't quite approve of her behaviour at times, but he did support her willingness to stand up for herself. Bishop Gunther on the other hand wasn't like most others in their faith; he was more lenient and accepting than most, always promoting change within reason. He insisted that households started using gas stoves instead of coal stoves. He had even arranged to buy a truck to help the community to cart goods to the local market in town. According to him, modern change to a bare minimum does not give the devil a foothold, it just shows the devil that they are capable of change without modern ways ruling their lives and changing who they are or distracting them from things that matter most.

Betty, much like Amity also had a strong personality, one she definitely got from her mother, but she also had a mischievous streak. When the elders instructed the children not to play in the rain, she was always the first to splash in muddy puddles. When they had their social events, she was the one who would pull pranks, like stuff a mouse in someone's pocket or stick a dish to a table cloth with workman's glue, causing a huge disaster when someone tries to pick it up. All innocent pranks at most, but that was how everyone knew her and more often than not, when she was younger her father would ground her for punishment, but she always found a way out of it.

And then there was Rachel, shy quiet Rachel. More like the runt of the litter, she was one of few words and always just tagged along because Amity and Betty insisted. Rachel only had a father; her mother died giving birth to her. Her father eventually married Elsa, a widow with two sons, who she never got on with. They were two brats and she ended up spending more time with her friends than her own family and over the years, the trio had become the best of friends

Betty giggled and Amity squirmed on the bale of hay, "I bet you David looks like that when he takes his shirt off," she said pointing to the male model in the fashion magazine.

Amity giggled, "It's scandalous! If your dad knew you had these, he'll shun us all," she said in jest.

Rachel, curious as ever, was sitting on the left, also peeking at the magazine, one of the few they kept hidden in the barn under one of the wooden floor slats. They always snuck to the barn to page through the magazines and weigh every other man in their town up against the likes of models that posed so shamelessly with nothing but pair of underpants on.

"*Jah!* Well he doesn't know now does he?" Betty said and paged through a few more pages.

Rachel would never admit it out rightly but she also felt a slight tingle of excitement when she looked at these magazines, they were not overly crude, but they showed more flesh than she had ever seen in her life. Maybe it was because of this, that they were all still single, she thought. Comparing the local boys to those men were like comparing apples with onions.

A sudden noise quickly alerted them and Betty shoved the magazine behind the bale of hay they were seated on. Both Amity and Betty grabbed their egg baskets, while Rachel stood around looking as guilty as ever.

"Betty, are you girls here?"

It was Betty's father who called, and Rachel's stomach lurched, if the Bishop had any idea what they were up to they will be in so much trouble.

"We're here *daed*!" Betty called and dusted the hay off of her dress, "We were caught in the rain, and was waiting for it to pass," she said as her Bishop Gunther appeared.

"I thought so, well I have come to get you girls home, the storm is a long way from being over," he said and handed each of them a rain coat, "Better we hurry, or the storm will catch up with us," he urged them as he let each one of the girls walk towards the barn door ahead of him.

The sky was dark and it wasn't just a summer shower, it was a downpour that looked more like a waterfall from heaven. Heavy drops struck the ground tunnelling into the earth. Up ahead stood the buggy, which didn't offer much or any shelter and Rachel wasn't so sure if they would make it to their respective homes in one piece. Betty was the first to step into the rain, followed by Amity. Bishop Gunther looked at her and nodded, and then in a huddled group the four of them ran towards the buggy, careful not to slip and fall.

Thankful that there was still some daylight to guide the way, the three girls clung to each other as Betty's father steered the buggy towards the house. Hardly able to see a few feet ahead of them and on a treacherous road that has been washed away in most places, Bishop Gunther was still able to make them feel at ease. He didn't even look worried, but then again, that was probably how a man of God should be, like Paul walking on water.

The buggy wheels rattled as they rode over rocks and muddy trenches formed by the mass of water running diagonally across the small road. And a trip that normally took less than fifteen minutes to travel, now seemed like an eternity. They were slowly making their way ahead through the stormy downpour, unbeknownst to Bishop Gunther, the road up ahead had turned into complete sludge and the moment the buggy reached it, the wheels simply slid into a deep trench on the side of the road, pulling the buggy, with the horse off and on to the side of the road. The girls screamed in panic as the buggy slowly leaned over to its side, threatening to topple over. Rachel was the first to clobber out and then helped the other two on to the road. Betty got out safely, but as Amity stumbled out of the buggy, she stepped in a hole and twisted her ankle.

"Ow!!" she cried out as she fell to the ground grabbing for her ankle.

"Amity!" Betty cried and ducked down to help her friend, "Where does it hurt?"

Bishop Gunther also hunched down and looked at her ankle, "It's quite swollen, I think you may have sprained it, can you try and step on it?"

Betty and her father helped Amity to her feet, but the moment she put weight on her injury, she cried out in agony.

"We will have to get you home, just lean on me and Betty" the Bishop said. He studied the state of the buggy, "The buggy will have to stay here until morning."

"But papa, we can hardly see in front of us," Betty lamented as she supported her friend.

"The Lord will light our way," Rachel said confidently and gave Betty a gentle reassuring squeeze.

With Amity supported by Bishop Gunther and Betty, and Rachel next to them carrying the egg baskets, they started down the path taking carful steps in the dark.

Through the stormy gale and rain that kept showering, they heard a galloping sound that sounded more like thunder coming towards them and the next moment, a man on horseback arrived completely drenched.

Rachel couldn't make out his face, but right now he was the best thing that could have happened to them.

"Bishop, Maryanne sent me to see what was keeping you," he shouted over the raging storm, "What happened to the buggy?"

Rachel took over from the Bishop, while he explained to the stranger exactly what had happened, and suggested that they come to recover the buggy in the morning once the rain has passed.

"Betty, you will have to get on the horse with Amity, Rachel you will walk with Uri and I," the Bishop instructed and then the stranger named Uri, helped Amity, and then Betty on to the horse.

Together they slowly made their way back to society, the first stop was Amity's house, where the Bishop helped to get her inside, and seen to, then it was Rachel's turn and finally Uri, Bishop Gunther and Betty made their way to the Bishop's house.

~*~

After Rachel had changed into her night dress and towel dried her wet hair, she deposited herself in front of the fire place. The night had turned out a complete disaster. She was sure it was punishment for their bad behaviour. Lusting like that over fictitious men and so on. She wrapped her quilt around her shoulders and reached for her bible. She knew better than to let her judgement be influenced by anyone. Despite the guilt, she somehow found her mind drifting to the stranger who came to their aid. She still couldn't see his face clearly, but she was sure he was handsome, and strong.

She shook her head to chase away the thoughts and closed her eyes, and said a silent prayer of repentance. She was never going to look at those magazines again.

Chapter 2

The sun broke through the parted curtains in Rachel's room and she pinched her eyes shut. The night before had taken its toll on her, and resulted in her oversleeping when there was still so much to do. She was yet to feed the geese and get ready to go to the local market to deliver the eggs she had collected the day before, but she simply had no will power.

"Rachel!" Her step-mother called from the kitchen, "Come have your breakfast!"

Rachel covered her eyes with her forearm and sighed. She just needed a few more minutes of sleep, but she knew where her priorities lay. She willed herself out of bed and rushed around the room to get ready for the day. By the time she got to the kitchen her mother had already cleaned the dishes, and Rachel's breakfast was waiting.

"The Bishop and his friend were here earlier," Elsa commented in passing, "Looks like you girls had a rough night."

"Yeah, we got caught in the storm," she mumbled.

So the stranger is one of the Bishop's friends, which means he was old, she thought to herself.

"Apparently Amity had twisted her ankle quite badly, but she will be fine in a few days."

"I figured. She stepped in a hole when she tried to get out of the buggy, we couldn't see much."

Elsa came to sit at the table with her, "You girls need to be more careful, things could have been a lot worse."

Sometimes Rachel couldn't help but wonder what Elsa's agenda really was. At times she treated her like a stranger, barely paying attention to her, and other times she came across all motherly. And all this time Rachel had no choice but to keep her own emotions all bottled up.

"We will," Rachel said and stood up to wash her plate, "I'm taking the eggs to the market, is there anything you need me to do?"

"Oh not to worry about the eggs, I've already sold delivered them this morning."

Rachel felt as if she could crush the plate in her hands. Those eggs were her eggs, her income. She was saving money for herself, and now Elsa had taken the little bit she could earn for herself.

"Thank you," she said tight lipped without turning around.

"I hope you don't mind, your father does need some money to buy that new gas stove so, I figured every penny would help."

"Of course," Rachel turned around this time, with a fake smile plastered on her face, "I'll just get more eggs to get money for my new dress."

"Why on earth would you need a new dress?" Elsa said with mock surprise, "Don't you have enough as it is?"

Rachel was slowly starting to lose her temper, but she fought hard to remain calm, "I only have three dresses, and I need one for church, the others are all worn and faded."

Elsa laughed, "It's not like you'll be catching anyone's eye, and you're past the point of marriage. You're already considered a spinster."

"I'm only twenty-two, the same age my mother married," Rachel protested.

"And see how that turned out."

Elsa had barely said the words when her sons, Caleb and Alfred came into the kitchen, and Rachel had to hide her anger. She simply scooped up her empty egg baskets and stormed out of the house. How that woman dared say such heartless things and get away with it, was beyond her she thought as she marched determinedly in no particular direction. But as the anger subsided, it was replaced by doubt. Maybe it was too late for her to marry, but then the same applied to Betty and Amity, they were both the same age. Obviously living in Derby Creek wasn't much help either, there were far more women than men here, and unless they had gatherings from nearby towns, chances of finding a suitor was slim.

First of all there was Betty, who insisted that she was waiting for Mr Right, she refused to settle for less, then there's Amity who also had her own ideas of a suitor, and the few men that did ask for her hand in the past, were coldly turned down because she was just not interested. Rachel always thought that Amity was the kind who would go on a Rumspringa if her father allowed her, out of the three friends, she was the adventurous one.

Rachel grunted a loud oomph as she collided with someone sending her baskets flying. Thankfully they were empty; otherwise they would both have been covered in egg yolk. She stumbled back and started to apologize profusely when she swallowed her words, and a pair of very strong hands cupped her shoulders.

"Are you alight?" the young man asked, and offered her a lopsided smile.

"Jah, I am fine, I-I wasn't paying attention, I'm sorry," she said struggling to breathe.

"It's quite alright, you were miles away there for a second, I'm Uri, Rachel right?" he said and released her as he tucked his thumbs into his suspenders.

Uri, the name immediately rang a bell. He was Bishop Gunther's friend, but how? He was so young, she wondered.

"How do you know my name?" she asked foolishly.

"I came to your rescue last night in the storm, but I suppose you won't recognise me, it was rather dark."

"Oh! Oh right, yes. Well... um, I'll be going now. Thank you, I mean sorry, I... I have to go."

Rachel just about ran away from him, she had acted like a complete and utter fool, stuttering over her words like a second grader having to do an oral assignment. No wonder she was single. She couldn't sit in the company of a man without feeling awkward. As she hurried away she could feel his eyes burn into the back of her, but she refused to glance back. The farther she got away the quicker her out of control heart and raging butterflies would quieten down.

"Rachel!" It was Betty who waved her down, "Where are you heading?"

"Eggs!"

"You're going to Eggs?" Betty giggled.

"No, ugh, I'm going to collect eggs silly," she corrected herself as Betty fell into step next to her, "How is Amity doing?"

"She's fine, but you look like you've seen a ghost, why are you in such a hurry," Betty said as she tried to keep up to Rachel's pace.

"I need to sell enough eggs to buy a new dress. The cow sold all the eggs I collected yesterday."

"What a cow, did she not even ask you?"

"Does she ever?"

The rest of the way, the two friends walked in silence, Betty on her own planet, and Rachel trying to get Uri out of her mind. She hadn't expected him to be so young, nor did she expect him to know her name. The night before was a bit of a blur with everything going on, and she mostly remembered walking beside Bishop Gunther while Uri guided the horse by its reins with Amity and Betty on horseback.

"Is Uri your..."

"Don't you think Uri is..."

They both said at the same time and then burst out laughing.

"Uri is so handsome," Betty continued, "The last time I saw him was when we were kids. His family has been in Germany for the past few years."

"I didn't expect him to be so young," Rachel said, "Are they staying here?"

"Only Uri, he's staying at our house and is helping papa with a few things."

Rachel could hear by Betty's tone that she was keen on Uri, and she knew by the seam of her dress, that Amity will be just as taken by him.

One of them will most certainly catch his eyes, she thought and smiled softly. Her friends or at least one of them deserved a good strong man to care for them.

She dismissed the notion of Uri straight away, knowing that she would never stand a chance. She could hardly string together a proper sentence when she bumped into him earlier.

Chapter 3

Amity humped along with a crutch in one hand, while Betty excitedly skipped besides them. For the first time in who knows how long, Betty and Amity had made some effort to look presentable, both of them had brand new dresses. It was the Friday night frolic, where most boys got to voice their intentions.

Betty was nervous; as usual she was shy and nervous. She never liked these events much, she did not trust the thing called love, her father loved once, he had promised his her mother that he would make sure she was taken care of, but now years later, all she had to remember her mother by was a single letter, and a lifetime of regret. Elsa was kind in some ways, but she was jealous of Betty, and Betty never did much right in her eyes.

The people from the surrounding farms started to arrive, old and young, in the middle of the big barn the table was set as always. Food in excess was spread across the table, along with lanterns casting a dim glow over everything.

"Have you seen how handsome Uri is?" Betty whispered under her breath.

Amity giggled and shifted in her chair, "I know right? I can still feel his hands on my hips as he helped me on to the horse."

"Oh and weren't they the biggest stronger hands ever?" Betty swooned.

"I'm going to make a play for him you know?" Amity murmured under her breath.

"No you're not, I am, and I've already spent some quality time with him."

Betty wagged her brows and reached for bunch of grapes.

"You can't eat now, we have to say thanks first," Amity said slapping Betty's hand.

"Oh please, no one is even looking."

Betty listened to her friends as they cooed over the newcomer and she opted not to show any interest. They had reason to try and win his affection, she had none. She will see this night through and make the best of a bad situation. Besides, she had a lot more on her mind. Maybe it was time she accepted the fact that she was a spinster, and she figured it was time she spoke to the Bishop and go his take on her moving out of her paternal home into her own. She could always offer her help as a teacher. She knew how to read, in fact she loved reading. She could go spend time at the local school and read to the youngsters, even help the school teachers to give extra lessons in literacy.

"Rachel!" Amity's voice broke into her thoughts.

"Oh... sorry I wasn't listening," she apologised.

"I was saying, maybe all three of us should play for Uri, we can see which one he picks."

Rachel raised her brows, "He's not up for auction, it's a silly game you're wanting to play."

"Stop being such a drab! It will be fun."

No it won't, she thought. The first thing that is bound to happen is that Uri will pick either Betty or Amity, then that will leave one or the other angry and disappointed, ruining a friendship of many years.

"I'm not a drab, I'm just saying. What if he picks Betty, then you'll be angry, not?"

Amity rolled her eyes, "You take things way to seriously, if he picks Betty, then so be it, I'm hardly desperate to marry."

"Come on Rachel, it will be fun; besides, maybe he shows no interest in any of us, then at least we know we all tried."

Betty worried her lip and looked down at her hands, "I don't know, I suppose no harm can come of it." She for one knew that she won't be the least bit phased if he picked Amity or Betty, because she knew she stood no chance.

Amity shoved her elbow into Rachel's ribs and gestured with her head towards the door. Talk of the devil, Uri was heading straight down the path on the opposite side of the table with his eyes fixed on them. And once again the sight of him made her heart race and as she watched him approach it was as if all else around her faded. She had tunnel vision and it was only him looking straight at her. When he finally stopped and took a seat directly opposite her she averted her eyes immediately. Of course, Amity kicked her under the table and Rachel cleared her throat uncomfortably.

"*Hallo* Uri," she said.

"*Hoe gaan het*, Rachel?" he smiled.

She only nodded, her tongue felt like led in her mouth, and her palms were sweaty.

Betty and Amity both fell right into conversation, putting their best foot forward while Rachel wanted nothing but to flee. Soon enough the evening got on the way, with youngsters all frolicking and enjoying the event. Uri made sure he mingled with everyone and never let on that he was interested in any of them in particular, which was funny, since Betty put her best foot forward and out rightly told him he had beautiful eyes.

As the evening drew to a close and most of the people had left, the last remaining few spent the rest of the time talking about the up and coming barn raising event. Uri was still seated across from Rachel, and Betty and Amity had moved closer to where Bishop Gunther was. He was playing the harmonica, which was probably the only instrument allowed in the community, but still sounded like heaven.

"So Rachel, have you always lived here?" Uri asked curiously as he picked on some of the bread sticks on his plate.

"*Jah*, I was born here," she said and offered him a shy smile.

"I'm surprised I don't remember you?"

"I'm not exactly the most memorable of all," she laughed.

"Oh but you are, you are a very beautiful woman."

Rachel blushed profusely and covered the side of her face with her hand, "Thank you," she mumbled.

"Can I pick you up for church on Sunday?"

Shocked at his request, Rachel shifted uncomfortably in her seat and worried her lip, as tempting as it was, she wasn't so sure if it was a good idea. But then again, Betty and Amity did say that they should all try and win his affection. She looked down at her empty plate and smiled. Perhaps it was time she stepped out of her comfort zone and tried dating at least, after all, he was simply going to take her to church, and it wasn't like he was proposing to her at all.

"Sure," she said and then got up, "I have to go now. I will see you around."

She saw his mouth open and close, but she rushed away regardless. She said her goodbyes to her friends and the rest of the community who were all still in the barn and headed home. Her mind was racing and her heart even more. For the life of her she couldn't understand what Uri saw in her. *You're a beautiful woman* – he had said, and it made her feel as if she was about to fly into the night sky on wings of angels. No boy, or man for that matter, had ever paid her such a compliment, and coming from someone as handsome and Uri, made her tummy do strange things.

Chapter 4

Uri was up and ready long before dawn on Sunday, making sure his buggy was clean and that he too was dressed in his best church clothes. He couldn't deny the fact that he felt bad for Betty, she had shown her affection so openly, but there was just no chemistry between them. Unlike Rachel, Betty was just too flamboyant to his liking. She was a pretty woman, but not even nearly as pretty as Rachel. Rachel was unusually pretty, with red hair that always seemed so perfectly plated and rolled up under her prayer cap, with loose strands that tickled her cheeks. The slight dusting of freckles across her nose, that spread to her cheeks made her even prettier, almost innocent not to mention the way she blushed every time he spoke to her.

He was quite surprised when she accepted his request to start off with, but pleased nonetheless.

The first night he saw the shy girl, with her baskets filled with eggs, he was intrigued. She was in control despite the stormy weather and their predicament, and even when he lifted the other two on to the horse, she never uttered as single complaint. She walked quietly next to them as if she was taking a stroll. Not even the rain slanting heavily against them broke through her composure. Maybe it was the way she kept to herself, or the way her eyes lit up the next day when he bumped into her, he wasn't quite sure himself, but if he had to pin it to one thing, it was God's will. It was God's will that he returned to Derby Creek after all these years and God had sent the storm so that he could meet his future wife.

"Uri, you're up early," Betty said as she entered the kitchen where he was having his morning tea.

"Jah, up and ready for church," he said and grinned excitedly.

She came to sit next to him and perched her chin on her hand, looking at him all dreamy eyed. Shifting slightly to get some distance, he smiled and shoved the plate of rusks closer to her.

"I'm on my way to collect Rachel for church," he announced, not sure how Betty would react.

From day one, she had made it no secret that she fancied him; neither did Amity, so it was better if he got it out in the open before either of them got their hopes up.

"Rachel?" Betty said scrunching up her face, "Have you asked her then?"

He nodded and took the last sip of his tea, "Jah, she's a shy one, but she accepted my offer."

Betty scratched her head and slumped back in her chair, and Uri could just imagine what thoughts were flitting through her mind, hoping that this would not ruin their friendship. But when Betty stood up and held her hand up for a high-five, he grinned.

"She's a dear friend, but a nervous wreck, you best make sure you treat her right," Betty grinned, "She's had a lot of hardship with that stepmother of hers."

Uri frowned, tempted to ask about this stepmother, but held back. If anyone was going to tell him about Rachel, it was Rachel herself. He would want for no secrets or tall tales to come from anyone other than her.

He looked at the clock against the wall in the kitchen and took his hat, nodded at Betty and headed out. For a man nearing his thirties, he felt like teenager himself.

~*~

Rachel waited outside for Uri's arrival and her stomach was doing wild flips, while her heart was missing beats every so often trying to keep up the pace. She had never entertained the advances of a man, and had no idea how to behave in the presence of one who had made his intensions clear. A boy simply did not offer a girl a ride in his buggy unless he was interested in her as more than a friend. This was serious business. She also omitted to let her father know, because she knew that Elsa would have a hundred and one things to say about it. She shifted on the swing chair changing her position, trying to find the one that made her feel most at ease, but her body felt awkward. Her arms felt as if they were too long, her legs felt numb and overall her body and mind appeared to be disconnected. Tired of trying to figure out the best seating position she stood up and paced up and down the porch, and then finally she opted for leaning against the pillar. Just in time too, as she heard the nearing rumble of a buggy, which could only have been Uri.

When he came to a stop in front of her gate, she quickly rushed down the stairs.

"Morning Rachel, you look lovely today," Uri said as he climbed out and came around to help her in.

"Good morning," she said softly.

"Did you sleep well?"

"Jah, I did, thank you."

It took her some time to loosen up and say more than four words at a time, but Uri had this amazing ability to make her feel free. With him she didn't have to count every word, or watch her tongue. She could just say what she wanted. On their way to church, he asked her about the things she likes most. The talked about her life, and her family, she didn't feel like she needed to hide anything from him at all. She even admitted how she felt about Elsa, which made her feel less restricted. At church, they didn't sit next to each other, but Betty and Amity were curious as ever.

"So he picked you did he?" Amity whispered under her breath.

"I don't know, maybe," Rachel murmured.

"You're blind as a bat; everyone can see he likes you."

Rachel blushed and kept her head down, her friends were impossible and as much as she tried to pay attention to the service she couldn't. If it wasn't for Betty or Amity, whispering to her under their breaths, it was the sure awareness of Uri watching her. And that did not go unnoticed by her friends either.

By the time the service had come to an end, Rachel couldn't wait to get outside to catch a breath of fresh air, and steal a moment for herself, but it was short lived.

"You never told us you're meeting a boy?" Elsa said as she came to stand next to Rachel.

"I didn't know I needed your permission," Rachel said blankly.

"Well I suppose you are old enough to make your own, but you know, Albert will be very disappointed that you never told him."

Rachel knew exactly what Elsa was playing at, and this time she was not going to let the woman who pretends to care throw any hurdles in her way.

"I think he'll live, and you should be too pleased that I won't be a bother to you for much longer."

Talk about rushing into things, Rachel thought as she hurried away from Elsa, it wasn't as if Uri was going to ask for her hand in marriage, they hardly knew each other. But even if that wasn't the case, whatever happened, come the beginning of winter, she would move out anyway and start her own life, with or without a husband.

Chapter 5

Uri had spent most of the time getting to know Rachel, and the more he got to know her, the more he was convinced that she was the perfect wife for him. He had spent almost every evening visiting with Rachel and in the past few months since they started their courtship he got to know a woman, who despite her adversities in life, rose above it all. Her stepmother no longer tried to boss her around, and her father was too pleased that his only daughter is finally blooming.

It was a perfect autumn day; the ground was covered in a carpet of reds and golds that reminded him of Rachel. He had already asked her father for her hand in marriage, and although it didn't quite follow the custom of dating for an extended period, he saw no reason to wait. They were both adults who were in love and certain of one thing, their own happiness.

As usual he waited patiently for Rachel to exit the house, and like two curious toddlers Amity and Betty was not far away either. They had both come to terms with the fact that he had made his choice, and they were extra supportive of Rachel too. As he whispered a silent prayer for guidance, Rachel made her appearance as if the Lord had answered his prayer. Today was the day he was going to ask her for her hand in person.

"Good morning Uri," she said and her smile lit up his world.

"Morning to you Rachel, you look absolutely radiant today," he complemented her and it earned him an even wider smile.

"I made myself a new dress, do you like it?"

"It's beautiful," he said and held out his hand.

He could already imagine the gasps and giggles coming from the two friends as he struggled to find the right words. He had rehearsed it so well, but now here in the moment, he was at a loss for words.

"Are you alright?" she asked and placed the back of her hand against his cheek, "You look flustered."

Uri cleared his throat and caught her hand, keeping it against his cheek, "I'm fine, but there is something I would like to ask you."

Rachel tilted her head and her hazel eyes sparkled with curiosity as she waited for him to speak.

"Go on!" Betty shouted from across the road!

Uri closed his eyes and smiled, they weren't helping him at all.

"Uri?" Rachel said softly, "What is it?"

He took a deep breath, and then took both her hands in his, "Rachel, I have spoken to your father, and I would be honoured if you would agree to become my wife."

The way Rachel's expression changed from being concerned to completely surprise was priceless. She didn't have to answer him at all, because the way her lips tugged into a wide smile and her eyes filled with tears, he knew she wouldn't turn him down.

Rachel flung her arms around his neck and buried her face in the crook of his neck and whispered, "I thought you'd never ask."

Uri chuckled, "I was hoping you would accept."

"Why would I not?" she said and smiled lovingly up at him.

JOANNA

1.

Tracing her finger over the cold, gray tombstone, Joanna inhaled deeply and choked back a sob. Kneeling in the pasture of their family's cemetery, she placed a bouquet of daffodils in front of the stone. It all felt like a dream to her. She didn't think she would ever lose her mother. She was her best friend and now that she was gone Joanna felt lost. She spoke softly to the stone just as she would as if her mother were standing beside her. "Hello, Mother. I miss you more each day. I really wish you could have stayed. It's lonely here without you. Everyone is trying to be strong. They want to continue life as it was before, but without you being here, it's impossible. I know you're in a better place and you're not in pain from the illness ravaging your earthly body, but it's still hard. I just don't know what to do now. I have assumed all of your household duties, just as you would have wished, but I find myself feeling increasingly empty. None of this feels right." Before she could finish her conversation, she heard the distinctive sound of horses clopping in the distance. She knew her brothers would be coming to take her back to their small home in the center of their community. They would have finished their errands in town, and she would be needed soon to start preparing supper. Dusk would be upon them soon, and after evening services, a good meal, a nice fire, and sleep would be arriving soon.

Joanna stood up slowly and ran her fingers along the cold stone one more time, giving a weak smile of recognition to her brother, Eli, who trotted up on his prized horse, Petunia. Petunia was a gentle creature and was easily broken. Eli was good to the creature and she respected him as well, she wouldn't ever buck him off, even when they were traveling through thunderstorms or if she ran up on a snake in the tall weeds. They trusted one another. Joanna could say the same about her brother, even though she was the older sibling, they trusted one another and vowed to always protect one another through all of life's trials. Eli looked down from Petunia and frowned. He hated to see his sister suffer so, but as a young man, he knew that for the good of the community he couldn't let his own sorrows show. He had to be strong for his sister now and show nothing but unconditional support. Now was the time for them to come together as a family and keep each other close. That's what his mother would have wanted. "It's good to see you, sister. Are you ready to return to the house?"

Joanna looked up at Eli's eyes and knew that behind the deep brown spheres, there was a touch of sadness that lingered there. He was trying so hard to put on a brave front, but she knew the truth, he wouldn't be the same after their mother's passing either. "Yes. I'm ready to return, Eli. Can I ride with you?"

"Of course. I think Petunia has it in her to walk us both back home along the path." The horse merely whinnied and they both laughed at her response. As they trotted along the path, Joanna's voice turned solemn once again as she asked, "How's father today?"

"He didn't say much at all, he merely got up and went into his study, where he read some scriptures and made some notes for service, then he walked out into the garden and surveyed the crops. It was like a typical day for him it seems."

"I wish he would express himself more."

"Ah, you know how he is Joanna, that's how he always was, stoic and stone-faced."

"Yeah. Maybe one day we'll figure him out."

"Ha! You have jokes, my sister. I seriously have my doubts about that."

They rode back up to the house in relative silence only listening to the sounds of the birds chirping and the echo of Petunia's hooves against the ground. Reaching the house, the pair dismounted and Eli walked Petunia to the barn, taking care to make sure she had plenty of fresh hay and water. Joanna went straight into the house and immediately made her way to the kitchen. In her mind's eye, she could still see her mother standing by the stove, stirring a pot or leaning over to get a knife from the bottom drawer. It was up to her now to make sure the family was fed. She sighed heavily and reached up above the family's ice box to take down a larger pot which hung above it. It was cast iron and the same one that had been used in the family for generations to make hearty stews and soups. That night Joanna decided she would make the family a hearty beef stew. They had some extra meat frozen already in the icebox and she had plenty of canned vegetables from the summer and fall's gardening. She poured some water that had already been carried inside into the large cast iron pot and lit the fire beneath their wood and coal stove. When it came to a full boil she added the meat and vegetables. Her mother had always tried to make her stews last for a few days and made it a point to ensure it was filling as well. Joanna added some corn starch to thicken the broth and proceeded to flavor it with spices. When her father walked into the kitchen, he hung his head, but then looked up and met Joanna's eyes, giving her a slight nod of approval. When the preparations were finished Joanna carried the pot along with some freshly baked bread out to the dining room. The family took their assigned places around the square table. In their mourning period, it was customary to set an extra place at the table for the lost as well, so her mother's chair while empty next to her father, had a place setting and was served some stew as well. It would be her father's task to consume it.

2.

After all was seated, her father spoke. "Good evening my son and daughter. Let us all rejoice and give thanks for what the day hath brought forth. Now is the time we must graciously give thanks for the abundance the Lord hath provided us with and draw close together as a family in our hour of need. I was reading the scriptures this morning and they brought me much comfort. Despite our loss, I trust each of my children to go on living and continue to be upstanding and show true grace. Now let us break bread and honor the fallen."

They all opened their eyes and lifted their heads watching their father who broke the first bit of bread. He then passed the plate to the others who took their portions and set the tray back in the center of the table. Their meal was eaten in silence and no one dared to speak until their simple supper was finished. Their father then looked at each of them and smiled. Tufts of white hair showed his age and he had a natural ruddiness to his skin tone that made him look jovial. He also had lines etched along his forehead left by the many years of being contemplative. One would look at him and assume he was a stern man all of the time, but he had crows feet and smile lines along his eyelids that told another story. While their father was stern and quiet, Joanna could remember a time when they were children he would play their games with them and tell stories which made all of them laugh joyously. He was a man dedicated to worship, but he also was a man who prided himself on the family he had created.

Rising from the table Joanna began to gather the dishes and place them in the kitchen sink, as she crossed into the other room she heard her father say, "Joanna, I'm very pleased with all the progress you have made in the kitchen with meal preparations. Your mother, rest her soul, would be very proud of you." Tears formed in Joanna's eyes and she bit her bottom lip to choke back a sob. Her mother, Annabelle, had been gone now for over a month, but the loss still stung. Her entire family was stuck living with the reminders of her being. Joanna still hadn't had the heart to clean out her closet or her sewing room. The elders had planned a town gathering at the end of the month, however, so she thought she would take them then and donate them. After all, she was a practical woman, just like her mother before her, and knew that there was no sense in good pieces of clothing going to waste when someone less fortunate could be using them. She responded to her father when returning to the table for a second trip for the remainder of the dishes.

"Thank you father, I appreciate it. I discover more techniques every day. I feel personal growth is important, don't you?"

"Why, of course it is, Joanna. I've watched you and Eli grow through the years and I'm proud of both of you. I personally feel comforted by the fact that no matter how many times I go to complete a task and fail, I always have another opportunity to give it another try. That's the beauty in salvation and forgiveness. As humans, we all fall short of perfection, but there's always the chance to redeem yourself through prayer and multiple attempts."

Eli cleared his throat and spoke for the first time since they arrived home. "I'm glad for that. I know that there have been many times I felt lost or like I was on the wrong path, but I would pray about it and then something would happen or suddenly change in my life." Joanna listened to the pair talk from the kitchen while washing up the supper dishes and smiled. She loved her father and brother dearly but felt lost. She had no one to talk about her daily affairs with now that her mother had passed. She couldn't tell her father about the gossip she overheard while getting notions for sewing. She couldn't talk to her brother about a certain feeling she had in the pit of her stomach when she watched the baker's son splitting wood while hanging their linens out to dry.

She listened as their conversation continued. Her father spoke in a good-natured tone and there was nothing condescending in his voice as he elaborated on the subject matter with his son. "Eli, do you remember that time you came home crying when you were thirteen or fourteen? It was late in the evening and mid-summer. You had just returned from Mrs. Hollister's barn dance, she was having to raise money for the local town orphanage. You came to me and had tears in your eyes and your lips were swollen and shaking. I'll never forget how dejected you looked."

"Yes, father. I remember that well. I had gone to the dance and got quite upset when I saw Pamela Davison dancing with my friend, James."

"Do you remember what I told you?"

"No, I can't say I can recall, though it must have worked, I haven't harbored feelings for Pamela since that night."

"What I told you then son, was that sometimes we think we know what's best for ourselves, but in the end, it's not us who is ultimately in control of that. Our actions may influence our day to day activities, but it is only through faith we can fulfill our ultimate destiny. Our almighty father wants us to be happy, but sometimes we have to learn a lesson the hard way so we don't pursue other things. Your courtship with Pamela, for example, is one of those things. Do you know what she's doing now?"

"No, father. I haven't a clue."

"She decided to go live among the outsiders. Her life has not been beneficial from it, given my understanding. The last news we received in a letter that she decided to pursue her career as a professional dancer. It turns out that career path led her to work in a nightclub for exotic dancing and she's developed a drug addiction. It's in my best estimation that she will more than likely spend a great deal of her life in prison for drug related crimes or prostitution. So, son, as you can see sometimes our Father doesn't answer our prayers for a reason."

"What if I could have changed her? If she stayed with me, then maybe she would have just lived her life pursuing the path of righteousness."

"Well, I know how susceptible young men are to the wiles of women and their charms. I think that given the choice, you would have left and gone with her and been corrupted by the outside world as well. Outside of our community, there is a temptation to pursue wrongdoing on every corner. No matter what your vice, there is some way to purchase it or attain it there. Never forget that on your travels, Eli."

"I won't Father."

3.

Joanna listened to their conversation while she continued to tidy up the dinner dishes. She knew that her mother would have loved that their father was attempting to socialize with his children, but she also knew that her mother would have played devil advocate in the conversation. She wasn't like most of the other women in the town. She was outspoken and often had heated debates on matters of faith or business with her father, yet they worked to balance each other out very well. Joanna was convinced that when God made her mother, his creation was done purely to spite her father and keep him in line.

She cleaned up the sink and then decided she would go ahead and get the percolator ready for the morning's coffee. She knew that would be the first thing their father would ask for when he woke up in the morning. He often preferred the strong brew first thing, then would go out to complete his chores, foregoing breakfast until their animals had been fed. He always said that if one took care of the animals, they would, in turn, take care of you. He lived by this strict routine day in and day out, with little variation in routine, save for the day he celebrated his wedding anniversary with his wife. On that day, both their father and mother would take a rare trip to town, where they would return with not only small gifts for the children but some goods, that were less costly to purchase such as new blades for the farming equipment. Joanna always dreamed of the outside world as being some type of magical realm where everyone had access to things like running water and life was easy, but as she grew older she realized the outsiders weren't much different than those in her own community. She wasn't allowed to do much traveling into town, but when she did she just noticed that the outsiders seemed to base their own value on their material belongings. This concept just simply didn't exist in her community, everything was shared.

Joanna saw that it was dark now outside and with her chores attended to, she didn't see the point in staying with the menfolk talking around the dinner table. Drying her hands on a dish towel, she decided to go ahead and excuse herself. Walking around the side of the table she approached her father and placed her hand on the side of his chair then leaned over kissing him on the forehead. "I'm going to go ahead and turn in for the evening, father. The nightly chores are all completed."

"Ah, yes, very good little one. My precious daughter. You have sweet dreams and remember that your father and brother are here if you have night terrors."

"Oh, papa. I love you. I haven't had a night terror, though, since I was seven years old."

"Still.. think good thoughts."

"I will. Goodnight. Goodnight Eli."

"Goodnight, sister, remember I love you even in your slumber."

"I will."

Joanna walked to her bedroom and lit the small candle that was on her nightstand, it provided enough light to read by, which is the only thing she enjoyed doing in the evenings to relax. Taking off her bonnet, she sat on the edge of the bed and began undoing the long braids she had in her hair. She preferred to keep it pulled up and away from her face during the course of the day since she was often doing chores. The tresses undid themselves easily and she fluffed hands through it, taking her hairbrush and running it through her long brown locks. After she put on her nightgown and hung her daytime dress back up in her standing closet, she picked up her Bible, seeing the notes she had made in the margins. She had been studying a chapter in Revelations that her father recommended. He felt that it would benefit the family to examine the reasons for death together, so they could make some sense of their mother's unexpected passing. She sighed and remembering her place decided she would finish reading and analyzing the chapter when she arose the following morning. Instead, she picked up the paperback she had borrowed from the town's library. It had a handsome cowboy on the front of it and he appeared in front of a herd of galloping horses. He was holding a blonde woman in his arms and she was swooning. Joanna smiled as the opened the book to the place she left off. It wasn't customary for women in her community to read much at all, but she enjoyed the thoughts of romance and found nothing wrong with dreaming about a handsome cowboy of her own. She finished the chapter and blew out her candle, reclining on her twin bed and closing her eyes sleeping almost immediately.

4.

As the dawn peeked through the clouds, Joanna was awakened by Eli, barging into her bedroom unannounced. He let the door bang on the hinges and had a panicked look on his face, as Joanna pulled the covers up over herself asked, "Why, Eli?! Whatever is the matter?! Is it Father?! Is he okay?!"

"Yes. Oh, Joanna, I'm worried. It's Petunia. She's fallen ill I'm afraid. Can you come out to the barn?"

Breathing out a sigh of relief, Joanna nodded and said, "Of course dear brother. Don't be fearful. The Lord will protect Petunia. Give me a few moments to get decent and I will be out there." Joanna calmly got up from her bed and walked to her closet, taking a few moments to pull her hair back and put on her bonnet then putting on her daytime dress. She pulled the laces tight on her boots and hurried out to the barn where she could see Eli standing by Petunia's stall pacing anxiously. "Thank you for coming out sister. I can't figure out what's wrong with her. She won't respond to my coaxing and she's just lethargic. I've never seen her in this state."

"Calm yourself, Eli. Your panicked state is doing her no good either. Animals can sense your fear." Joanna walked up to the mare who was laying down and looked into Petunia's deep brown eyes. She then placed her hand gently on the creature's forehead. She then stroked the animal's head and back, making soothing sounds, just as her mother would do them when they were sick youngsters. "Yes. You're right to have come to fetch me. She's definitely fallen ill. Let's just hope its a bug. Father has a trip planned to go into town to gather some new ax blades for the fall cutting. I'll go with him and stop by the library and see if I can find a cure in some of the veterinary medicine books they have shelved. Don't worry, brother. We will do what we can for her. Just be fervent in your prayers and there will be a way delivered."

Joanna walked back into the home and began preparing her father's morning coffee. Daylight had just broke and she knew he would be happy to get the day started like normal. When he walked in the kitchen he smiled seeing her standing at the stove as her mother would have, fixing his coffee and preparing breakfast for her brother. Eli always had a voracious appetite She set the steaming mug in front of him and said, "Good morning, Father. I must confess it's already been eventful."

"Oh, really how so?"

"It seems Petunia has fallen ill. I was hoping it would be okay if I went with you while you were in town today to look up some medicine for her at the library."

"I certainly hate to hear that Petunia has taken a turn for the worse. She has been good to our little family. I think that's a wonderful idea darling. God can work miracle cures, but only if we're willing to do a bit of the work as well. After the morning feeding, we will go into town. Be prepared. While I'm purchasing the new blades for the fall wood harvest, you can look into a cure for our Petunia. I bet your brother is worried sick."

"Oh, he is Father. You know he's always been close to the mare."

"We shall do what we can. Thank you for the finely brewed cup of coffee. Now I must get to work, the daylight is already streaming upon us and the chickens will be happy to receive their breakfast."

"Thank you, Father."

Joanna finished making the biscuits and gravy for breakfast then poured them all glasses of freshly squeezed orange juice from the assortment of oranges that they had traded for in town earlier in the summer. She knew their shelf life would be expiring soon and didn't want anything to go to waste. Waste not, want not, her mother always said. She also knew that they all need to keep their strength up because as soon as they got back from town the entire community would gather and chop wood for their collective heat in the winter. After completing her chores and cleaning up the cooking utensils she set the meal on the dining room table and gathered her bag for their trip into town. She made certain she had her city library card and decided to take her paperback with her and exchange it for another as it was nearing completion anyway. Looking around the empty room she sighed. She was worried about her brother, but also she felt a doubt creeping into her soul and a generalized discomfort, wondering if this is how the remainder of her days would be spent, taking care of her father and brother , never knowing the love of a man or having her own family to raise.

Her father and brother came back into the house after feeding the animals and sat down at the table, nodding in appreciation at having their meal already set before them. Eli spoke then, asking to say the morning prayers and included a blessing for his favorite mare as well. They ate the rest of their meal in silence and Joanna immediately went to the sink and began cleaning up the dishes, so she wouldn't have to do both the breakfast and dinner dishes before bed. She also was anticipating having a busy day tending to Petunia upon their return. Her father came and got her when the horses were hitched up to the wagon and her brother helped her climb in beside him. Her father gave his horses a quick pat on the head and they departed on their journey into town.

5.

Arriving in the nearest town, Joanna took in her surroundings as her father hitched up the wagon to the hitching post by the hardware store. She got out of the buggy, amidst the stares of the townspeople. She imagined she looked quite strange to then in her pale blue day dress, with her hair pinned up in a bonnet, while her father was dressed head to toe in all black, complete with his wide-rimmed black hat. His long brown beard wasn't shaved, merely groomed and it did betray his age, as spots of gray could be seen in it when the sun hit it just right. He spoke briefly to his daughter before going inside the store. "Remember daughter, be polite to the townspeople, but do not engage in lengthy conversation unless it pertains to spreading the Gospel. I will be here when you are ready to leave but try to find the information you seek quickly. I suspect this lost time will hurt our productivity later and we won't be able to get as much done as we should. Be careful, Joanna."

Joanna nodded and hugged her father before crossing the street and rounding the block heading to the library. She cast her eyes downward mostly only looking up periodically to dodge obstacles. She opened the doors to the city library and the pleasant librarian smiled and waved at her when she entered. She smiled back and returned the greeting. She liked the librarian, who never questioned her when she came in even as a little girl clutching her mother's skirts. The older clerk would give her lollipops when her mother checked out her religious books and romance novels. Now Joanna was grown and even though she didn't get a lollipop, she still felt those warm feelings when she was in the library. She walked up to the desk and quietly dropped her book on the counter. "I need to return this, and I will be getting another one if I can find the other information I need in time."

"Sure thing, Joanna. Have you been doing okay, since your mother's passing?"

"Oh, yes we have been doing alright, thank you. I'm sorry I was in such a bad state when you saw me last. I am adjusting to this new normal."

"Well, that's good. If you need anything, you let me know as always."

"I will. I will see you when I return."

Joanna then walked off, smiling once more at the clerk. She rounded the corner to the reference desk where there was no clerk, but there was a younger looking man in grease-stained coveralls standing by the finance books, looking bewildered. Joanna watched him pull out a book from the shelf as the rest came tumbling down. She couldn't stifle a small giggle as he fumbled trying to catch them all. He turned around hearing her laughter and she was met with a sheepish smile and the most striking blue eyes she'd ever seen. He took her by surprise as she felt her heart beat faster within her chest and suddenly heat rose to her face as she blushed deeply. Before she could say a word he smiled broadly at her and said, "They don't make these shelves the way they used to do they?"

Joanna giggled once again and said, "No. They certainly don't."

"I don't really know much about this place. I needed a book on taxes, I own my own mechanic shop and I'm doing my own this year to save money for the business. Maybe I should have just paid someone."

"Well, what are you looking for? Maybe I can help."

"A book to tell me how to do it."

Joanna paused for a moment surveying the shelves then reached down to the bottom one, accidently brushing the man's hand as she picked up a hefty volume and placed it in his arms. "Here you go. This will guide you through the process."

"Oh wow. Thank you. I appreciate that ma'am. It's nice to meet you, my name's David."

"I'm Joanna. I'm not from around here, as you can tell."

David took a step toward her, closing the distance, and Joanna felt a certain electricity pass through them. She let the heat rise to her cheeks again and once more looked into his blue eyes. He was in good shape and looked strong from his work. He had blonde hair and was clean shaven. He didn't look like any of the men from their community, but he did seem to possess the same kindness behind his eyes and good spirit. He responded by saying, "I wish you were from around here. I'd hire you to do my taxes."

She chuckled at his joke, then suddenly remembered her purpose. "I really hate to cut on conversation short, David, but I have to get some information then return to my community, my brother's horse is sick and needs medical attention I know nothing of."

"Oh, I'm sorry to hear that. Maybe I can help. I grew up on a ranch."

She couldn't believe her ears. She had wanted a cowboy all of her own. Could it be that her prayers had been answered? He seemed so genuine and caring. She explained the problem with Petunia and David gave her the information she needed to attend to the mare. He reassured her it was nothing major that some tender loving care couldn't fix. He then went on to say that his specialty in life was fixing broken things. Joanna considered the gravity of his statement before turning to leave and decided to do something she would need to ask forgiveness for later.

"You have been so helpful David, could I have your address?"

"Only if I can have yours too."

The pair exchanged addresses and Joanna exited the library, turning around to see David staring at her making her exit. She didn't know what had come over her, but she knew in her heart this man was her destiny.

6.

She exited the library to find her father standing red-faced by the door, checking his pocket watch. She hadn't realized how much time had passed talking with David, she only knew that it felt like they had known each other a lifetime. Feeling the need to apologize she spoke to her father, when they crossed to the buggy, "I'm sorry, father. It took me longer to get the information I needed than what I thought."

He didn't say anything, but merely nodded and coaxed the horses out of the lot and towards the path back to their community. Her father finally spoke when they were close to the halfway point between town and their village. "You know why we caution each other when talking with townspeople? It's not because our religion has restrictions on being social and making friends. In fact, we are encouraged to witness to everyone we possibly can. It's because not all people are righteous, Joanna. Not everyone will have your best interest at heart, and the original evil does find its way into the hearts of men. Some of the people you encounter in the outside world, well let's say the majority of them, only are interested in preying on the weak. It's their life's goal, not helping others or doing good."

Joanna turned her eyes downward again as her father patted her on the leg continuing, "Remember, no matter what happens, Joanna, your family will always support you within the community. We, however, could not help you should you decide to live among the outsiders. You would be shunned and on your own, you know it's our way, there's no changing that." Joanna nodded in acknowledgment, silently rubbing the piece of paper in her pocket which had David's address on it. She knew in her heart, that she needed to see the mysterious cowboy mechanic once again, but didn't like the idea of her father's disapproval. He would never allow such a thing, she felt conflicted and sick at heart the entire way home.

Arriving back at the community they were greeted by Eli, whose worried look had only grown more exasperated during their time away. "Greetings, Father. Greetings, Sister. Did you acquire the knowledge you sought?"

"I did brother. Let's go to the barn and see what we can do."

Together they walked to the barn and checked on Petunia. Joanna took care to follow David's precise instructions and administered a careful mixture of salt brine and water to the mare who greedily lapped it up. It had seemed that she had just gotten a bit dehydrated during their previous days' activities and was feeling under the weather. They monitored her condition throughout the day and it did improve as she eventually got up and started wandering back and forth in her stall, anxious for a trot. In addition to that the new blade purchase, expedited the wood cutting process and the community made short work of the wood pile, stockpiling enough wood to last the entire winter in half the time it normally would. They decided as a community to celebrate their recent accomplishment and give thanks to the Lord, with a feast to be held that upcoming Saturday night.

Joanna spent the night quietly in her room after supper and allowed herself to think of David. She knew beyond a shadow of a doubt that she needed him in her life. She believed, despite her father's warnings that there were good and decency in his soul. No one without a good heart, would have freely given her that information she needed to help her animal. Most of the outsiders would have offered their services and charged a pretty penny for such knowledge. Joanna thought of the feast Saturday and sighed. Did she want to be stuck in the community all her life, eventually marrying a man who had little passion for anything in life? It was then Joanna made her decision. She would slip away during the barn dance on Saturday and go see David.

As the community was abuzz with the festivities at the dance on Saturday night, Joanna excused herself to go back to the house, hugging her brother and her father tightly before exiting, saying she felt ill and needed to call it an early night. Unnoticed by anyone else in the community, she then proceeded down the well-worn path and made her way to town. She made her way to the address David had scrawled on a ripped piece of an envelope from his coveralls and knocked on his door.

David opened the door, rubbing his eyes, apparently awakened by her rapping. He was groggy but smiled broadly in recognition. "Joanna, is that you are am I dreaming?"

"No. You're not dreaming, David. I'm really here." She paused a moment, considering her options. She thought for a moment about what advice her mother would give her in this moment. She thought back to when she was a little girl clutching on to her mother's skirt, frightened by some imaginary threat. She would have said, "Ah, my precious little girl, there is nothing to be afraid of but your own imagination. If you don't give your fear power over you, you can achieve anything you want in this lifetime." Joanna hesitated a moment then said to David all while blushing and smiling, "I came to be with you David, and hopefully one day be your wife."

David took Joanna by the hand and led her over his front stoop, making sure she didn't trip over the door sill on the way in. When he shut the door behind her he pulled her into his arms and kissed her deeply. Joanna felt a joy like none other she had felt in her life, spread through her bones and body. He then looked deeply into her eyes and said, "Well. I'm not the smartest man you will ever know, nor will I ever be the ideal of perfection, but I promise you this Joanna. I am a decent man with a good heart, and I promise to make this life the best we can possibly have together. So, yes. I do want you to stay with me. You're all I've thought about since I met you that day at the library, and you're all I want to think about for the rest of my days." The pair then walked hand in hand into David's modest living room where they sit side by side on the sofa, holding each other until they drifted off peacefully.

SILENT SMILE

JASMINE FLOWERS

This is not a love story. You will not be told about how cupid runs around with an arrow filled with love. This is a tale of two hearts intertwined by fate and sealed by the forces of nature. Call it a sweet romantic story, but love is not all sunshine and rainbows. Love is a divine feeling that can create paths in the ocean and loopholes in the time frame. But also it hurts just as bad as death.

Annie Fisher was the third born in the family of five, two boys and three girls. Two of her older siblings had gone through their Rumspringa and had accepted to follow the church's faith. She was also expected to follow the same path as her older siblings. However, she always wanted more than the simple life she was raised into. She imagined what the outside world beyond Pennsylvania would be like she had a wild imagination and an adventurous spirit.

For years, Annie used to go to the woods and escape her simple reality. There was this abandoned house deep in the woods near the river. Sometimes when rain caught up with her, she would seek refuge in the abandoned house. Mary Fisher, her eldest sibling, had gone for her Rumspringa and when she came back, she accepted the Amish faith.

"Mary, can I ask you a question?" Annie asked her when they were in the barn cleaning.

"You always ask too many questions, just do the work we are here to do I have other chores to finish before dad and mom are back"

Annie never took no for an answer, "What was your Rumspringa like? What is the outside world like?"

Mary sat on a stack of straws and beckoned her sister to sit next to her. She told her that the outside world was cruel and cold. Everyone lived for themselves and people did not help out one another like in their community. There were a lot of bad people, and the ones that pretended to be nice were just foxes hiding in sheep's skin. Then Annie asked her if she had found love while she was on her Rumspringa. Mary looked down, and for a minute Annie could see that her sister was sad and wanted to breakdown. Mary answered with a simple nod and said dad raised us in a perfect Amish faith and I would not want to disappoint him.

Later that night, Annie sat on the side of her bedroom window and gazed at the sky. "It is so big and beautiful I bet there is so much to see out there maybe even find someone that will love me," Annie whispered to herself. She loved her parents and tried to be the perfect daughter that every parent could dream of. Her father used to tell her that she will get the best Amish man that will love her and they will have gorgeous grandbabies. She had decided that she will go to her Rumspringa then come back and join the Amish faith that she was raised in and known her life.

One day as Annie was locked in her room reading a novel about "Secret Desires of a Forbidden Love" her elder brother, Jacob Fisher, walked in on her. The two had a major argument about the novel, and the brother threatened to punish her. Annie then ran from the house and went into the woods. While she was walking to her secret hiding place, she noticed that the abandoned house had been cleaned and the bushes around had been cleared. The broken windows were fixed and the door had a lock. She wondered who had taken their time to do all that work. She was curious and tip toed towards the house to see if there was anyone home. When she peeped through the window, she saw the rooms were cleaned, but there was no one home. She walked away in a hurry so that however had decided to invade the place will not get her there.

When she reached her spot by the river, she climbed her favorite tree. While on top of the tree she saw some clothes by the riverside but there was no one around. Then when her curiosity was just about to tell her to see whose clothes they were, a man surfaced from the water. He had this strong physique but she could not tell exactly who it was because the vision was a little blurry. She knew what she was doing was wrong, but it felt so good and right. The man wore his clothes and disappeared into the woods as Annie remained hid in the branches. She did not know who it was, but she wanted to see him again.

Later that night Annie could not get the image of the naked stranger out of her head. She went to sleep with a smile of what had happened.

The woods were dark and the cold pierced through her skin, Annie had lost her way back home. The further she tried to get her way back home the deeper she went into the woods. The loud thunder sounds and lightning made her beat profusely. She was lost, and she did not think she could make it through the night. When she thought her night could not get any worse, she started hearing wolves hauling, and the sound was closer each time louder than the last. She did not have any strength left in her to run. She had given up on everything. A wolf appeared before her ready to rip her apart, and she knew her time had reached. She said a silent prayer, and before the wolf could attack, a man appeared and killed the wolf with his bare hands. It was the naked stranger from the river. He carried her in his, and before she could look into his eyes, her sister called her. It was all a dream! Even though it was supposed to be a nightmare, Annie thought it was the most beautiful dream she had ever had.

Days went by, and each day Annie went to her secret spot hoping she would see her handsome stranger again. It was more than a week, and there was no sign of him. Annie wanted to maintain the hope that he would see him again, but part of her knew he wasn't coming back. "I wish I could see him on last time to thank him for saving me from my nightmare," Annie silently spoke to her soul. On her way back, she saw lights on in the deserted house. She went and knocked to see who was living there, but no one answered the door. When she peeped through the window, she saw pieces of art and a there was one canvas on a painting stand but it was covered with a white sheet. She was curious to know what hid behind the covered canvas but the doors were locked.

A month went by, and she had not seen her handsome stranger nor had she visited her secret spot. Then one day as she was going through her closet, and she saw the novel that caused a fight between her and her brother. She hid it in her pocket and went into the woods to read it in her secret spot. On her way, she bumped into her handsome stranger. He was tall, his dark hair reflected the sun off it, and his blue eyes pierced through her heart.

"Hi, are you lost?" her handsome stranger spoke in a husky voice.

"No I know where am going except now you are standing in my way" Annie replied with a cheeky shy smile.

"I am totally sorry Miss."

"You can call me Annie, Annie Fisher,"

"Nice name. I am Leo Freeman; I used to hear my parents call me that"

Annie smiled and thought to herself that the man was super good looking and had a sense of humor.

"So what is such a beauty like you doing in these woods all alone? You know the woods can be quite dangerous."

She blushed and her cheeks almost turning red said it all. She remembered her dream and got lost in her fantasy world.

"Annie? Are you ok?"

"Am sorry. I was thinking that it's getting late and I should probably get home."

"Do you live out here alone?"

"I think it's a good idea you should go home. Pleased to meet you Annie" he said while walking away.

Annie stood there confused if she had said or did something wrong. She walked back home but could not get Leo of her mind. She tried to fill the gaps in her imagination of where Leo might be from. She had noticed that Leo's accent was different so he could have come from somewhere else. That night she went to bed, but she could not sleep. Who was this mystery man that she was growing so fond of, and she barely knew him? She worked up and sat on her bedroom window. She gazed at the sky and into the woods. While staring into the woods, she noticed a light. It was probably something burning. Although it was faint, she could tell that it came from the abandoned house. She wore her coat and with only a nightdress on she went into the woods. She knew it was a dangerous and a crazy idea. But as long as Leo was near that fire she was determined to solve the puzzle of her mystery man.

Leo had lit a fire to burn all the dry leaves and dirt that he had compiled while cleaning his home. "Who is there?" he asked after he heard wrecking sound of dry sticks. He pulled out a gun and pointed at the direction which the sound came from.

"Please don't shoot me," Annie said with a terrified voice.

"Jesus! You don't sneak on people like that. I almost shot you thinking you are a bear"

"Are you an orphan or something? Why are you here at this time?"

Annie was still terrified by the thought that she almost lost her life by being mistaken for a bear. She slowly composed herself and walked near where Leo was seated.

"Do bears exist in these woods?" Annie asked while still trembling.

Leo took the blanket that he was covering himself with and covered her with it. "There are no bears in these woods, but that does not mean that I should not be cautious."

"Why did you come out here at this time?"

Annie did not know what to say and she diverted the question. "First, I am not an orphan I have both parents, and secondly, you have to apologize for pulling a gun on me."

"I am sorry for almost shooting your beautiful face and calling you an orphan,"

Annie could not hide her flushed cheeks even with the cover of the dark. She explained that she had come into the woods because she thought that the house was burning. She asked Leo what he was doing in that house that was abandoned for many years. Leo was not comfortable talking about himself. He knew that he wanted to share his story with someone he just wasn't sure if Annie was the one. When he hesitated to answer her question she figured it was something that he was not comfortable sharing.

"You will talk to the trees and your bears if you do not start making some friends," she said hoping to lighten the mood.

"I am not very good at interacting with people."

The night was long, and the two talked about anything that crossed their mind. Leo felt comfortable with Annie and decided to share part of his past with her. Leo's parents isolated themselves from the Amish community after they had refused to follow the Amish faith. They were then shunned from the community and became an outcast. They build a home in the woods, but life was not very bearable, so they decided to move from Pennsylvania to West Virginia. Leo was the only child and was raised there. His parents died when he was 17 years old and lived his life raising himself. He was an artist and used to paint peoples' portraits at a corner shop.

He later joined the Army where he served as a radio operator. During the Gulf war, half of his unit died in the battlefield. This had a significant impact on Leo because most of them were his friends. He decided to start a new life after the war, but he did not have enough money. So he opted to go to his parents' original home in Pennsylvania. He did not have much to go by because when they left, he was a small kid except for the photos and stories that he was told by the parents. Annie felt his pain as he talked about his life and she could not take any more.

"Am glad you are here now" she spoke as she hugged him.

The hug came as a surprise, and he did not know what to do. It had been long since someone had shown him such affection. He hugged her back, and she felt his heartbeat beating. She slowly closed her eyes as they made the hug tighter. The fire was burning out, but the moonlight graced the moment. She looked into his ocean blue eyes and time stood still, the glitter of the stars shone in eyes. He held the back of her neck and drew her closer towards him. As her lips were closer to his, she could feel his warm heavy breath soothing the surface of her lips in the cold night. He softly kissed her lips, and she could feel the blood run into her stomach. It was her first kiss.

"It is almost dawn, you should go home" he whispered into her ear.

Time went by first, and even though they wanted to spend more time together, they knew it was impossible. They were worlds apart and trying to create anything between them would be like stirring an active volcano. Leo walked her to the edge of the woods, and as she walked away, he could not get enough of her. He was tempted to go after her, but he knew the repercussion that it would have both on of them.

Annie reached home and climbed over the window. She laid on her bed and touched her lips softly reminiscence about the kiss. She was losing herself to the world she knew nothing about. On the other hand, Leo could not sleep and continued with his painting hoping that Annie would show up again. The following day Annie woke up very early and started cleaning the barn and doing other chores. By the time the rest of the family was awake she had done almost her daily chores.

"Dad I want to go and see Sarah," she asked her father's permission to leave.

"It is fine my dear. Make sure you come back early."

Sarah was her best friend, and they knew each other since they were little girls. They shared most of their secret and fantasies together.

Annie walked away, and as soon as she was by herself, she diverted into the woods. It had only been a couple of hours since she departed with Leo, but it felt like she had not seen him forever. She ran as fast as she could because no matter how much time she had with him it will never be enough. When she reached Leo's house, the door was unlocked, but he was not home. She made herself comfortable and started snooping around. While she was on it, she saw Leo's painting, and she was fascinated by their beauty. She remembered there was art on a stand that was covered the last time she saw his pictures. She went through each piece, and she saw a painting of a girl peeping through the window. She was shocked at the perfection of the art. Looking closely at the painting it was a painting of her. Before she could finish going through the painting, Leo walked in.

"I see you have made yourself comfortable."

"I figured if I stay outside you may shoot me thinking am a bear."

The two laughed as they hugged each other tightly.

"I missed you so much I could not wait to come see you"

"I am glad you came, I could not sleep, and so I did this" he was talking as he unveiled a painting that was covered on the painting stand.

It was a painting of the two kissing in the moonlight. The painting almost made Annie burst into tears. It was the best thing that anyone had ever done for her. She had spent most of her life trying to please other people. She had not gotten that much attention but she never thought it was a problem.

Leo wanted to open up his past completely to Annie. He took her to his bedroom where the paintings spoke volumes about his past. The room was cozy, and the dim light set the mood right. There was a painting on the wall of older folk; she thought that must be Leo's parents. Other paintings were of soldiers and landmarks of different places. Truly Leo's paintings exposed his pain and happiness in life.

Leo took her hand and lightly kissed the dorsal side, he knelt down before her and asked her if she would be part of his story.

"Leo what are you trying to ask me?"

"I want you to be part of my story. I want to start a new happy chapter with you by my side."

"Leo I would love that. But most guys are after sex and short-lived pleasure. How will I know you are not that kind of a person?"

"I will wait as long as you want Annie."

She could tell his honesty as his sky blue eyes were transparent as ocean water. She could see the tears from his eyes through his eyes.

"I promised myself and God that I will not do anything until marriage."

"I could not agree any lesser with you."

The two talked for hours and Leo shared hidden parts of his story. They danced and sang in the moonlight. They were the only people that existed in their world. It was the first time that both of them were purely happy. He did not know how to express himself in words but he surely did perfectly with his painting. Leo wanted to express himself the best way he knew how.

"Can I ask you for a crazy favor?"

"I have had enough surprises for today but you can ask."

"Can you please pose for me, I want to capture this moment with my art."

"Leo, did you severely hit your head during the dance?"

"I am serious Love, I don't have words to express this moment, but I know art will."

Annie's cheeks flushed and her hazel eyes bright. It was then that Leo realized he had just admitted he loved her. She agreed, and Leo positioned himself at an angle that allowed the moonlight to flow on her body while her glossy completion brightened the room.

She had the beauty of Venus and a chiseled body like the Aphrodite, the goddess of love. Her blonde hair fell her shoulders, her arched eyebrows graced her heavenly smile, and her glossy skin complexion drew all the energy from the room. Beauty would be an understatement of how Leo described Annie in his mind. He stared at her for long without saying a word then he turned to his converse and started painting.

She maintained the same pose while staring at Leo. It was then that she realized that Leo had the body structure of a gladiator, his hard-predatory ocean blue eyes were soft and deep when she looked at her, and the ridges formed in his body by muscle definition made him look phenomenal.

Leo was good at what he did, and soon he was done with the painting. He covered it with a piece of cloth and told Annie he would unveil it to her but not at that time. Annie did no insist on it and knew he had a good reason why he wanted her to wait. Time had flown, and Annie knew that she has to pass through Sarah's home to get an alibi. The two felt that they were losing pieces of themselves when saying goodbye. They lived in two paths separate from each other, and they could not travel both paths together unless one gave up their path and followed the other.

Annie reached Sarah's and found that she was in her room knitting a sweater. That was their hobby, and most of the time when they were together they would knit and share the designs.

"So you are knitting without me?" Annie spoke in her usual jovial voice.

"Annie, what a pleasant surprise. I did not know you are coming I could have gotten more wool," Sarah spoke while hurrying to hug her friend.

It had been long, and the two friends had a lot to catch up on. They had also planned that they would go for their Rumspringa together. "I need to tell you something, but you have to promise not to tell a single living soul," Annie said with a changed tone.

"You know you can tell me anything."

"I have a boyfriend."

"Whaaat!!!!"

"Sssshhhhh keep it quiet, or someone will hear us."

"How? What happened? Who is it?"

"You are asking too many questions at once. He is not one of us he came to town recently."

Sarah still shocked, she never thought that Annie could fall in love with an outsider especially with her father's position in the church.

Annie confided in her best friend about her secret love with a stranger. She knew she could trust her because they had been friends since they were little. Sarah always wanted to find someone who would treat her special. They talked and laughed at the funny moments together, and then Annie left for her home. The two promised not to pile up any more secrets between them.

Life was a fairy tale for Annie for the next couple of months she was like living in a perfect dream. She had found love and love had found her too. The man was like a replica of an angel that was sent to protect her from unhappiness and loneliness. She would sneak from her home at any time of the day or night to see Leo. He also grew courageous and sometimes he crept to their barn in the middle of the night, and they will spend hours together. One day Leo almost got caught by Annie's sister, but he hid well in the straws. It was the secrecy, adrenaline rush, and waves of romance that kept this couple together. They lived for the moment, and none of them wanted to talk or think about the future because it was scary. All the little things that they did Sarah knew about it, and to some extent, she started growing jealous of her friend and her new found happiness.

We all have secrets that we die, and only our lifeless hearts and souls would know about. Sarah had a big one, and she never opened up to her best friend. She wanted what her friend had. She was sleeping around with Jacob Fisher, Annie's elder brother. The two had their relationship long before Annie thought it was possible for her to fall in love. Sarah and Jacob kept their relationship a secret because Jacob was engaged to another woman. Most of the time the two would meet in Sarah's home barn.

One day during Sarah and Jacob encounter, the two had a fight. Jacob was breaking things off with Sarah because he was getting married soon.

"After everything you have put me through you think you can just dump me like trash?" Sarah complained bitterly.

"I never loved you, and you knew I was engaged" Jacob retaliated firmly.

"The first time you forced me to have sex with you, Jacob. You promised me that you would leave her and marry me."

"I love my fiancé, and I will marry her. I have my family's reputation to protect."

"If you care so much about your family's reputation then why do you allow your sister to sleep around with strangers?"

Jacob was furious and grabbed Sarah's neck "Tell me what you are talking about before I choke you to death right now."

Sarah tried to fight Jacob off her, but she was too strong for her.

"It is Annie; she is in a romantic relationship with an outsider."

Jacob stormed out of the barn furiously and headed home. On his arrival, he went straight to Annie's room and kicked the door open. Everyone in the house was shocked and ran upstairs to see why there was so much noise.

"Jacob what do you think you are doing," his father asked with his heavy accent.

"Annie has been deceiving all of us. She is sinning with an outsider"

Annie was at Leo's place while all this was happening. She did not know that her beautiful secret was now known by the whole of her family.

Leo had renovated their family's house into a beautiful home. He had put a proper fence and painted the entire house. He had finally gotten the new start in life that he wanted and had found love to grace up all his blessings. Annie had come that night with a puppy meal to surprise Leo with. In one of their encounter, Annie told him about puppy meal, and he refused to believe it exists.

"Wow! The meal was delicious; I almost ate my fingers in the process" Leo complimented Annie's cooking.

"Am glad you like it because I would have felt guilty if you did not."

"Why would you feel guilty?"

"Because it was puppy meal."

"oohhh…you must be kidding me."

The two were inseparable like the Greek gods Castor and Pollux. Annie had a jovial personality, and this made Leo fall in love with her more.

"You know that you possess the prettiest smile the world has ever seen?" Leo spoke with a faint soothing tone.

"And do you know that you inspire the prettiest smile in the world because my smile comes out only when am with you."

"I am immortal when I am with you because you stole my heart and I still breathing for you."

"Water and bread cannot nourish me when I thirst for your touch, voice, and site. You paint my scars and drain away my pain."

They talked, and when it was almost dawn, as usual, Annie prepared to go back home. They kissed and promised to meet later in the night. As she walked, she stopped and turned "Leo, I wish one day we will enjoy the sunrise together."

As her routine, she climbed through the window, and when she jumped into her room, her father switched on the lights. She was scared and confused; she wanted to jump back through the window and run back to Leo. Her father was a leader at the church, and she knew things would end badly for her.

"You have to go church and confess your sins if you still want to be part of this family" her father spoke with a sad tone.

"Father, Leo is not a sin. He is the man I love."

"You have to also get an Amish man and get married if you still want to call me father."

Her father's words ripped her whole being apart. They had judged her wrongly before they even knew her side of the story. She had not been intimate with Leo but everyone assumed that she had. She had never asked for much but the little she is asking she's being denied. She was being made to choose between her family and Leo. She did not want to pick by there was no other way out. Jacob had already suggested an Amish man that would marry her. She cried, but her tears could not drown her pain. She locked herself in the room for days and never spoke to a living soul.

Leo got worried because it was unlike Annie to stay away for so long. He thought maybe she had traveled or her relative was sick. He could not bring his mind to grasp what was happening. The days were longer and the nights unbearable. His heart was bleeding and his sanity tormented.

One night, he was in his room reminiscence about the times he spent with Annie, and it hurt more as he got deeper in the memory lane. He woke up, put on his clothes and went to look for Annie. When he reached the edge of the woods, he saw Annie's home, and even though the idea was crazy, he was determined to meet Annie again. He climbed to Annie's bedroom window and knocked. When Annie came to the window, and he saw it was Leo she quickly opened the window and went to fasten her bedroom door so that no one finds him.

Annie's glossy complexion was pale, and her bright eyes were turned dull. Her usual jovial personality was turned into a weak self-pity creature.

"Are you out of your mind?" Annie asked in a worried tone still looking around if anyone had seen him.

"Yes, Annie. I am insane and lifeless because you took both my heart and sanity and disappeared"

"Leo you have to go now, you cannot be found here."

"I am not going until I know what is happening to us."

She told him that her family had found out that she was seeing an outsider. They told her to choose between him and the family. They had also brought a man to their home and introduced them. The man was going to marry her in a few weeks. Leo was filled with rage, and it consumed every beauty from his eyes. He had enough of life taking away the people he loves and cared about from his life. He felt trapped in the evilness of life. He did not cry, but his tears soaked his chest. He did not have words to describe his pain.

"Can I see you one last time?" Leo asked with a shaky voice.

Seeing Leo again poked the deepest depths of her pain. They family did not just restrict her body, but they also enslaved her soul. She gave a simple nod to say yes to Leo's proposal. She watched as Leo walked away and disappeared into the dark. Her life, happiness was so near, yet it seemed so far from her reach. She went to bed full of tears. She did not want to be shunned away by her family and community. But this was not the life she wanted, and now she was going to spend the rest of her life with a man she barely knew.

A week passed, and Annie was ready to meet Leo the last time as promised. She waited for the dark, and she ran to the woods. She did not know why she was going, but her body kept walking towards Leo's place. She knocked on the door and Leo came with a bathing robe. He was just from taking a bath.

"Hi, I did not think you will make it."

"Leo you know the position I am in. I do not have any options."

"Then why are you here if you do not have any option?"

"I don't know" she did not want to say how much she had missed him.

She was offered a seat and a cup of coffee. The house was a bit messy, but no one wanted to talk about now.

"I am selling the house and moving to New York."

"This is your family home! Why are you giving up on it after all the work you have put into restoring it?"

"When I came here I thought I could start a new life away from the pain that the world has caused me. But now this place carries the most precious and painful memories of my life."

She started sobbing weakly "You don't have to leave"

"I love you Annie, and I cannot stay here while you are growing a family that could have been ours."

"The buyer has already confirmed the purchase, and soon I will be leaving."

"Leo, what do you want me to do? I will be an outcast if I disobey my family."

"Then come with me. Let's all leave our paths and start a new journey together."

The emotion in the room clouded their hearts, their minds, and all they could see was the pain that they were being subjected to. Annie stood and slowly walked towards Leo. She sat on his lap and buried her face on the side of his neck. Annie's tears soaked Leo's neck. He pulled her and looked into her eyes.

"Come with me, honey. You belong by my side."

They tried to fight nature's power by avoiding direct eye contact but their tortured souls were too weak to resist one another. That night, they become one again under the protection of the moonlight. They laid on the floor and talked about what their future would have been together. Leo gave her the painting that he had drawn the first time he asked her to pose for him. It was a picture of her, but she was pregnant, and Leo was in its background. "I planned to give it to you when you got pregnant with our first child." Leo had included her in his story through the painting. They were so close yet felt worlds apart. Although, she knew that her family will never accept them but what they had was so good like a sin dressed in a wedding suit.

This was a perfect life that she had also pictured, but now it was not possible. Her heart was bleeding as her soul claimed for clemency. They did not want to say goodbye, but it was almost dawn. Leo walked her to the edge of the woods. "I wish I could say that I will see you again but the decision is all on you" Leo spoke with a calm voice.

Annie disappeared into the dark on her way to her house. She could not sleep and kept thinking if staying was really what she wanted. She did not have much time as Leo would be living town soon. She was afraid of her parents' wrath that the same time she did not want to lose the man she loved.

Leo sold the house and gave out all the legal documents. He had lost hope of his love coming back. He packed his things and waited for dawn to catch a bus to New York. The bus was almost, and Leo stood in the dark waiting for the only bus that went to New York. The night was cold, and he was freezing. Suddenly he saw the bus approach. He looked back at the city he was about to leave, and the pain that came with the thought was intense. The bus stopped, and he hopped in and got his seat. Then when the bus was about to leave a strained woman's voice shouted: "Please wait for me." It was Annie Fisher. Leo quickly yelled for the driver to stop the bus and Annie got in.

Annie had run from home and choose to leave with Leo. She left a letter for her family apologizing for her decision. They were finally going to spend most of their mornings watching the sunrise together. Leo looked at the painting of them and looked back at Annie and the silent smile made the cold night warm.

END

THE YEARNING OF AN AMISH WOMAN

58

ERICA FENTON

Most days, Sarah Graber would have discounted the butterflies in her stomach as a new adventure awaiting. Something was to be explored and she should go look for it! However, this was a whole new stage in life. She had just taken on the teaching job in her Plain community and though she was thrilled about this newfound independence, she couldn't shake the feeling that somehow she was making a mistake.

"Oh, don't worry about it, honey," her mother consoled as she helped her fix a lunch for her first day. With three daughters, Elizabeth Graber always made a point to ensure that each of them felt special in their own right. Whatever they wanted to do, Elizabeth was their biggest supporter, along with their father, Jacob. Sarah knew she meant well, but she simply smiled and gave her mother the look that stated she was going to worry regardless of what was said to try to calm her.

"Thanks Mama, but that doesn't make the feeling go away."

"Well then you'll certainly have to rethink if you really want children or not. Consider this training for when you have children."

As much as Sarah had grown up wanting a family, she was becoming more unsettled with the idea of even watching her newborn niece when the time came. Being the second-born daughter, Sarah had made her sister Mary the promise that she would watch her children if the time ever came. Mary's little girl Lydia was now 8 weeks old, and though Elizabeth thought that was much too soon for Mary to let the small child go, Mary knew it was time for a break. It was decided that by the end of the first week of school, Mary would give Sarah her first official babysitting job so that she and her husband could go out for a small date.

As Sarah was driven to the schoolhouse by her father—who rarely talked before noon—she seemed to gain more actual butterflies based on the unknown of the coming day. And she hated the fact that she had no idea what to expect on her first day of school.

Most of the children who showed up were children she had seen at church or even at *Rumspringa* gatherings each week. Sarah had always been vocal about the school system in general, even in the Plain community, so many of the older children were surprised to see her, what was even more surprising was that they kept their comments to themselves. At least for the time being. Sarah was sure she would hear about it later, just like she had heard about it from the preacher and the bishop when he had come down to interview her for the job.

"Are you sure this is a good fit for you?" The bishop had asked with an eyebrow slightly raised. The answer had been no, she wasn't, but it was either become a schoolteacher or leave the Plain lifestyle behind altogether. She didn't seem to have much interest in the simple way of living, and had expressed as much to her parents on more than one occasion. They had responded by giving her more things to keep her mind from dreaming. Or so they thought.

"Yes, sir," Sarah had responded to the bishop, knowing that she would likely be stuck in this town with these people teaching children for the rest of her life.

The bishop had looked her over curiously for a moment before nodding his head and giving his approval, on the condition that she share weekly updates with the preacher. Why they thought she wouldn't, she had no idea. That was part of the job description, but she had this feeling that they weren't trusting her like they normally would had she been anybody else.

She was promptly brought back to her present surroundings when a stray paper airplane swiftly collided with her head. Most of the children laughed except for the culprit and his friends. Little William Gingrich had a tendency to cause more trouble than most, and immediately Sarah knew he was going to be the problem child this year. But at least she knew she would be here for the rest of his schooling. Or so she thought.

"Mama! Papa!" Sarah's little sister Hannah squealed as she ran into the house for supper. "David Zook asked me to court him!"

There were exclamations of what's and when's and how did it happen's but Sarah had no real interest in these affairs. She knew she should be happy for them. Hannah had been interested in David since they were in kindergarten together almost 12 years ago, but it was only recently that they both discovered how deeply they truly cared for each other.

All Sarah knew was that she didn't have a real desire for marriage. It was good for her sisters and her parents and the rest of the world maybe, but it just didn't seem like something she wanted. For her mother's sake, she tried so hard to want it. But being married seemed like a lot of work to Sarah, much like being Amish.

Sarah tried not to use that word around the people of her community that much. They preferred to be called Plain, while the rest of the world was called English, but in her mind she had always seen the Plain as what the English world would call them: Amish. The rest of it was the real world, and that seemed like the best explanation. She knew she was supposed to love her community, but she had never really developed any deep ties. The only people she would truly miss if she ever left would be her family... and maybe Isaac Ellis, who she had developed a liking to, but nothing that seemed to click. Sarah always saw herself being friends with Isaac, but nothing more. She almost felt bad because she felt like she was leading him on... but he was an extremely patient person, and that was one thing she loved the most about him.

"Sarah! Sarah!" Hannah bound into the front room where Sarah was sitting and quickly thrust her hand in her older sister's face. "Look!" Upon Hannah's finger was a gold ring with a small diamond set into it.

"Where did you get that?" Sarah asked, knowing the answer already.

"David Zook gave it to me as a promise ring that we will always be together, even if we're ever apart." Sarah gave her sister a look.

"And why would you ever be apart?" Hannah sighed, exasperated with the lack of enthusiasm from her older sister.

"We're not together *now,* are we? He's at home telling his parents, and I'm here telling you! Why aren't you more happy for me, Sissy?"

"I am happy for you," Sarah defended herself. "It's just been a long day since today was the first day of school. I'm just a little tired, that's all." She smiled and rose from her seat to give her sister a hug. "I love you, Hannah, and I'm so proud of you." She pulled back and looked Hannah in the eyes. "I am so happy for you and that you've found someone to spend your life with."

Hannah smiled, nodded and pulled Sarah in for a final embrace before racing off to the back of the house to find their mother and start discussing her "next move", as Mama liked to call it when she would talk about courting with her girls. Almost as soon as Hannah whooshed out of the room, Sarah saw her father round the corner with an eyebrow slightly raised.

"You're tired from school, eh?" He knew that Sarah's personal stance on marriage and the struggles she had been having as of late with deciding what to do. "You know, no one in this family would be upset if you wanted to leave this community. Even if you wanted to leave the Plain life behind. *Rumspringa* is a time to find out what it is that truly makes your heart free to be itself. Maybe you just need more time before school goes into full swing."

"No, Papa, I couldn't," Sarah looked out the window briefly and watched two robins twirl around each other, fighting for what seemed to be a worm. She shook her head as she looked at her father. "Besides, Mama would be upset. In fact, I don't know if she'd ever forgive me."

Papa stepped into the room fully now to give his middle child some love. Sarah was always a daddy's girl and soaked up every minute she could with her beloved father. The best thing she loved about spending time with her father was learning how her Heavenly Father worked in His Kingdom. How she was royalty no matter what she did or felt.

She had authority in places that most people only dreamed of. Papa would tell stories of great adventure for bedtime and although Mary and Hannah wanted to skip to the parts where the princess was saved by the prince, Sarah wanted to hear of how the princess learned to do things the way her father had always intended for her to do those things. She wanted to hear what it was like, telling a servant to do this or that and watching them move at her every beck and call. That was a power that Sarah wanted... but Papa said she already had it. All she had to do was ask the Heavenly Father to show her how to use her queenly authority to get things done.

But now, standing in the front room with her father by her side, she felt so small and fragile. Like a little girl who got lost in the castle and there was no one around to lead her back to the main corridor.

"Remember how you used to tell me stories of the princess and what is was like to be royalty?" Her father nodded. "Well now, I just feel lost in this great big castle and there's no one there to lead me back to anything familiar." Tears blurred her vision, but she thought she saw a shimmer in her father's eyes as well.

He smiled as he said, "I'm here now, my princess. I won't let you get lost again."

Sarah fell into her father's arms and they wept for a long time. No matter what happened, she knew that her father would always be there to bring her back to the place of sanity.

The rest of the first week went by without much more incident. By Friday night, Sarah felt like she was ready to take on anything, including watching her newborn niece. Mary and her husband Mark came over and brought diapers and a Pack-n-Play they had bought from an Englisher passing through who had seen they were pregnant and felt the need to get rid of some of their children's items. Although the Amish used cloth diapers, Mary and Mark decided they were going to use disposable diapers until Lydia was at least 4 months old. Sarah didn't mind using them though, she almost preferred disposables since it kept down on the smell in the event that Lydia had a poop explosion and being around just two months old, that's exactly what she had. Sarah was glad for the extra wipes that Mary had packed, as well as the fact that her parents did not, in fact, go anywhere for the night like they had promised. They helped Sarah clean up the mess and clean up the baby, and while Sarah got to hold Lydia most of the night, at some point she finally gave up on trying to get her to sleep and handed her off to Elizabeth, who effectively had her sleeping within seconds.

"It's all in the energy you give off while you're holding her," Mama explained in a soft tone while still rocking the sleeping infant. Sarah sighed tiredly and laid her head back on the couch.

"I'm beginning to think I don't want children, but at this point, I haven't even found a man." Elizabeth looked at her second daughter briefly before resuming rocking.

Finally she asked, "What do you mean? I thought you liked Isaac Ellis."

"Sure, I do. But I don't see myself being a wife to him or being able to live with him for the rest of my life."

Sarah's mother simply nodded her head thoughtfully and said nothing. After a few minutes, she got up and laid baby Lydia down in the Pack-n-Play and quietly left the room.

Sarah knew she should probably go and talk to her about what she said. Maybe she should expound on the idea or explain what she meant by the fact that she didn't see Isaac as a potential mate. If there's one thing she didn't want her mother thinking, it was the fact that she wasn't even interested in guys. That simply wasn't the case. She found men extremely attractive, but she wasn't sure that getting married was something she could do.

After arguing internally with herself, she quietly left the room Lydia was sleeping in and moved into the kitchen, where both of her parents were quietly sitting at the kitchen table. Papa lifted his head and looked at her as she walked in. He didn't smile, but his eyes had a certain glimmer to them. Mama was facing away from Sarah when she walked in, but as she moved around the table, she saw that her mother had been crying. Her heart broke at the sight, and she found there were suddenly tears in her eyes. She sat in the chair across from her mother and to the right of her father.

This is going to be an interesting meeting, she thought to herself.

Mama spoke first. "Papa tells me you've been debating getting married for a while now."

Sarah caught her mother's eyes and looked down. She simply nodded.

"I'm not upset that you don't want to get married," Mama continued. "I'm simply disappointed in myself that you didn't feel comfortable enough to share with me, but you felt comfortable enough to share with your father."

"He never told you?" Sarah looked up between her mother and father. She had a newfound respect for her father, who had kept her secret all this time. "I thought a husband and wife shared everything."

"So did I," Elizabeth shot a look at her husband but he ignored it, instead looking at Sarah. He simply smiled.

"Just because we share everything doesn't mean I'm going to share someone else's feelings for them." He spoke in a low voice, but his words were not minced. He took Sarah's hand in his and gave it a squeeze. "I cannot share *your* feelings about something effectively. I knew you would have to share with her and *you* knew you would have to share with her. You are now an adult and you can make your own decisions. *Rumspringa* or not, Mama and I only want you to feel comfortable with every decision you make because we know that whatever you choose will only have been thought about and prayed about more than anything else anyone could ever do in their life." His smiled deepened in a new way, as if he was remembering something.

Papa wasn't wrong though; Sarah sought the Lord about literally every decision she made and she wouldn't leave her prayer closet if she didn't think she had the right answers. Because she knew she was a princess, she would wait until she knew beyond any doubt what the Lord wanted her to do. She had never felt that release with anything having to do with Isaac or her relationship with him, and she'd even lost a full night's sleep waiting up for an answer that still didn't come. Sarah didn't know if the non-answer meant she needed to keep moving toward Isaac or away from him, so she simply sat in the valley of indecision and decided to hold Isaac at arm's length for now. She had also talked to Isaac and told him what she felt about the situation, and that's when he mentioned that he would be willing to wait if necessary. Somehow, Sarah still had this feeling that he would be waiting a really long time.

The days at the school went by quickly as Sarah did enjoy teaching more than she thought she would. She grew to love each of the children individually, even little William Gingrich, who still threw paper airplanes in her direction from time to time. As soon as Christmas rolled around, Hannah was already engaged to David Zook, so Christmastime was filled with planning the wedding and sewing dresses. Hannah knew how Sarah felt about marriage in general, but still made a point to involve her. At least that's how it felt to Sarah. She did enjoy helping her little sister prepare for the biggest moment of her life, especially since Mary had kept Sarah out of so much of the process.

Sarah always thought her older sister was prophetic, but it wasn't until she did something like exclude Sarah from any preparations that she realized Mary must know that she had no desire to get married. And why should she? She still hadn't found the "one" and though she had been with Isaac even during the time of Mary wedding, she never really felt comfortable with him by her side.

"Sarah, you have to stop overthinking. My dress is going to be as tall as you!" Hannah had put Sarah in charge of sewing the last few inches of her dress by hand. She had wanted that special touch, and she wanted her favorite sister to do it, she had said. Sarah held up the bottom of the dress and inspected it. She had gone a little long, but she also knew Hannah would be wearing heels. She shrugged.

"You'll be alright," she nonchalantly quipped as she grabbed the dress by the top and put it back on the hanger to return to the bag Mama had set aside for it.

Hannah huffed. "I don't want to be 'alright' for my wedding, Sissy! I want to be perfect."

"That's something I never really understood though. If David loves you for who you are, then why go to all this trouble to try to be someone you're not for a day?"

Hannah gasped as Mama walked in the room.

"What's the matter?" Their mother asked, curious as to why Hannah was inhaling so much air.

"Sarah thinks I'm becoming someone else for a day to marry David."

"Sure you are," Sarah replied defensively. "You're putting on a dress you'll never wear again with heels you'll never wear again for 20 minutes of your life so that you can marry a guy. I feel like there are different ways to go about getting married."

"There are and you're right," Mama paused while Hannah did more gasping. "However, when it's done this way, it is a reminder to us and to everyone watching that we need to continue to strive to be that spotless bride for Christ when He returns for the Church. The act of marriage is purely symbolic of the picture that John the Revelator painted for us in Revelation. Besides, some people like to get all gussied up for their wedding day." Mama winked as the girls both smiled at her. Elizabeth Graber did always have a way with words that made everyone else seem more at ease about life. "Now," Mama broke the moment by clapping her hands together. "We need to hurry and finish this so we can be done and get dinner ready. Mary and Mark are coming over tonight, as well as Isaac Ellis. Sarah Ann, you are going to decide tonight whether you want a relationship with that man so he can move on if necessary."

Sarah never had a chance to argue with her mother because as soon as she said that she whisked out the door and was gone. Hannah giggled and Sarah's face flushed. In that moment she realized she was never going to be more than friends with Isaac Ellis.

Just a few hours after Sarah and Hannah had finished the preparations on Hannah's dress and Elizabeth had them help her with dinner, Mary, Mark, Isaac, and David came over for dinner at the Graber's. Since that first night that Sarah babysat Lydia, she had found that she actually really liked the little girl and was glad she was the first one to babysit her. She said as much to Mary, but Mary just scoffed.

"Unless you go somewhere, we planned on you being the only babysitter for the rest of her growing up years."

When she heard that, there were suddenly butterflies in her stomach again. That unfamiliar feeling that said she was going to experience something new soon. She hoped that something new didn't involve Isaac. Sarah stopped herself. Did she really just think that?

During dinner all seemed to be going well. It was nice to have a full house again, plus a few extra guys for Papa to talk business with. Sarah had to make this announcement before God and those she would call family.

"I would like to say something, if that's alright." She had interrupted a deep debate on the best way to use squash in a dish when everyone stopped and looked at her. The butterflies suddenly multiplied and intensified. She decided to take a drink of water, which helped, but only slightly. She turned to look at Isaac.

"Mama told me tonight was the night for me to decide whether I wanted us to pursue each other or not. I know this probably should be kept between the two of us, but I trust each one of these people around the table and know that they will support my decision, no matter what it is." She paused, trying to read his face but he was keeping it completely blank. "I have decided that I do not want to pursue a relationship with you. Not because I don't like you, but because I feel like I'm only holding you back." She stopped, looking for the right words. "Every time I try to envision us being together, I feel like that wouldn't be optimal for us. We've talked a lot over the years; I know that we don't have the same dreams and goals in life. That would make any relationship difficult right from the start. I'm sorry, Isaac. I hope you won't hold this against me."

Everyone around the table was quiet for a few moment, but Mary broke the silence first.

"I always knew you weren't cut out for marriage, Sarah. That's why I didn't want to make you be a part of something you had no interest in doing. Mama told me later there were other ways I could have gone about showing you or telling you that it wasn't that I didn't like you or thought you would mess anything up. I just didn't want you to do something that you weren't passionate about. And really, I'm glad that you finally told Isaac how you really feel. It's better that you are open with each other, even if that isn't what either of you want."

Many around the table agreed, but Isaac just remained quiet. Eventually he started eating again, but Sarah could tell by the way he was eating that he was only doing it for show. She was sure he had lost his appetite, much like she had trouble even finding one before this meal. Before dessert was even presented, Isaac excused himself, thanked Mama for the food and promptly left. Sarah knew him leaving before dessert was the biggest sign that she had just broken his heart and her heart broke for him... but at the same time she was glad to finally let him go. Maybe now he could find someone that would make him truly happy and they would live together forever. In some ways though, Sarah felt like another tie in her life was cut. It was making it harder to stay in this community, or even to stay Amish.

Thinking of that brought on a whole new bag of questions that she didn't even know existed until this moment. Like what was she going to do in the real world? What kind of jobs would she get? Would she meet someone? What if she met someone just like Isaac and fell in love with him even though she had rejected Isaac? Would she be able to live with herself then? Why couldn't she just be happy for herself and her newfound freedom in not having a guy that was waiting for her to make up her mind?

For the rest of the weekend, that last thought kept her up every night.

It had been a week since she had told Isaac in front of her family that she didn't want to pursue a relationship with him. She hadn't seen him once in that time. Not even when she walked home from the schoolhouse everyday and walked by his field. Not even at church where he would normally sit... or anywhere in the church for that matter. Thost butterflies that normally resided there turned into a vacuum and she was starting to think that maybe Isaac had done some harm to himself. Everyone seemed to act as though it was business as usual, and even Mama said that maybe he was just trying to get over a broken heart.

"You guys have been together for a long time," her mother's words comforted her some. "Even if you weren't officially courting, you had been considered an item to be mirrored by many of the younger ones in the community. You had always kept your relationship open, clean, and friendly. Everyone liked to use you as examples whenever they would talk about the way dating should be." She rubbed her daughter's back. "If something happened to him, I'm sure we would have heard something by now."

"I just want to apologize to him," Sarah said plainly. "That's all I want to do. I want him to hear that I don't hate him and I really do wish that he finds someone." Her mother was quiet for a minute before responding.

"Why don't you write a letter to him? Tell him he doesn't have to respond, but let him know how you truly feel. Papa and I know how you feel because we watched you grow up. Mary knew how you felt because she had seen how you would roll your eyes at any weddings we went to, even when you went to your own sister's."

Sarah looked at her mother and realized she was right. She could just write a letter to Isaac. "But I really want to know what he thinks."

"Then tell him at the end that you would like him to write back!" Elizabeth laughed. "Don't let this keep holding you back. The reason you let him go was so that you could both fly."

Sarah decided to wait until the last day of school to write to Isaac. It seemed like an eternity, but she wanted to make sure she had the right words. She also wanted to make sure she was focused only on the letter and what she wanted it to say.

That evening after dinner, Sarah wrote the letter.

Dear Isaac,

I hope this letter finds you well. It's been a long time since I've seen you and I've been very worried about you. I do still care for you and want to see you succeed. I was hoping we could still be friends, even if there's no hope for a marriage type relationship between us.

Maybe I should explain myself a bit too. Growing up, I had never really had much of a desire to get married. Being from the Plain community, marriage is the only real course of action for a woman to take... but I always felt there was something more there than just getting married, having children and dying. I want to go on an adventure. I still do, in fact! When I say that we don't have the same dreams, I already know that to be true because I know you want to stay here, but I want to travel. I want to see the world and all that it has to offer.

<u>I know that I'll miss my family terribly and I'll miss you terribly, but as long as your desire is to stay here, then my desire is that you find someone who has that same dream as you and you hold onto her with all you are. She will treat you right and make sure that you are well-cared for and have many children.</u>

<u>Sincerely,</u>

<u>Sarah Graber</u>

Sarah looked over her letter and knew it wasn't going to replace any face-to-face conversations she wanted to have with Isaac, but maybe it would help him see things from her perspective. Since she had put in the letter that she wanted to travel and leave the Amish community, she decided as she sealed the letter that it was time to tell her family as well.

That same night after dinner, Sarah gathered her parents and Hannah in the front room to tell them her plans to travel. Everyone was very quiet, but her father was the first one to rise from his seat and extend his arms. Sarah melted into his strong arms, sobbing as she did. That wasn't the response she was expecting, but she knew it was her father's way of blessing her. When she pulled away, she saw that her mother and sister also had tears in their eyes, but they had smiles on their faces.

"Ever since we knew that travel was something you wanted to do, we've been saving up money." Elizabeth pulled out an old, wooden box from underneath the chair she was sitting in. "We know it's not much, but it will at least get you started."

"Never settle for second best," her father looked at her sternly. "The world out there is hard and cruel. Never lose that sense of wonder that you have for God's creation."

"Always search for the cheapest ways to get to the next place and don't drink the water in other countries," Hannah said these things as if she knew they were true. Everyone looked at her curiously as she put her hands up. "I read it in a book somewhere!"

They all laughed, and that laughter was exactly what Sarah needed. She really was going to miss her family, but she was glad that they were willing to let her go.

Sarah decided she wouldn't leave until she was given a proper good-bye from Isaac, but that meant she had to hunt him down. On a Saturday morning, most men went to the home restaurant of Isaac's aunt Priscilla's, and Sarah had this feeling that she would find Isaac there as well.

As soon as she walked in the door, she saw him. He was sitting at the first table inside the doors reading what looked to be like her letter. She could tell he was at the end because he kept turning it over expecting to see more. She marched over to his table just as he looked up to survey what was going on in the room around him. His face went pale when their eyes met, but she could also see there were tears in them.

It had been a little over a week since she had written the letter and exactly a week since she had sent it. She was glad to see it had gotten to him and said as much as she sat down and Aunt Priscilla came over to take her order. She decided some coffee, eggs and toast would be great since she was there and sitting down, then she turned her attention to Isaac. He looked to be in no mood to talk, but they were going to because Sarah had things to say to him. But before she could say anything, he interrupted her.

"You know, you think you know people so well... and then they go and write you a letter and you realize you don't know them at all." He looked at her, but only to make eye contact. Sarah could tell he was only getting started. "I have fought and prayed for you for *years* knowing that you were the one God was sending me. I knew from the moment you said hello to me in church my first real day there that God had sent you into my life. You may not realize this, Sarah, but just because you can live without me doesn't mean I can live without you. When I think about my life without you in it, I don't even see a point in living. I don't care whether you've had a desire to see the world or not. I'd go anywhere with you, do anything with you... as long as you're by my side, it doesn't matter where I am."

Sarah was shocked. Of all the responses, she had guessed she would get, this one was never on the list. She told Isaac as much and he only laughed. But it was almost a sad laugh.

"Sweet little Sarah has her life all figured out. How does a guy even stand a chance when you won't even let anyone into your life to give them one?" Isaac had tears streaming down his face now, and Sarah found that her face was wet as well. "I would go to the ends of the earth for you, but you won't even let me walk you to the end of the street on a rainy day."

Sarah was at a loss. "Isaac, I—"

"No, Sarah. I'm done with your excuses." He wiped at the tears on his face. "When are you leaving?"

Her heart squeezed. "Tomorrow... after church."

"Then I guess I'll see you at church tomorrow." With that, Isaac stood up and walked out of the restaurant,

Sarah cried the entire walk home. In fact, she didn't even remember walking home. She simply remembered being there as her father ran out to meet her and grasped her in one of the strongest and most loving hugs she had ever known. They stood out there and she cried into his shirt, soaking the spot where her face was. She was sure she had felt some drops on her head, but when she looked up, she only saw her father smiling.

"My dear Sarah. Always living up to your namesake. You know that you're a princess and you know what you want. Maybe you should stop trying things your way and try one more thing before you leave your father's house forever." She looked up at him, confused. "Go get the boy! He loves you, Sarah, and he's not kidding when he says he would go to the ends of the earth for you."

Sarah furrowed her brow. "How do you know he said that?" It was then that Sarah saw tears in her father's eyes.

"Because the same night that you told him you didn't want anything to do with him was the same night that he had told your mother and I that you were his everything and he wanted to be with you."

The next day at church Sarah could hardly sit still. She was eager to leave, but not before she actually saw Isaac one more time. She had cried the entire day away and knew if that was going to be her life, she'd rather have Isaac in it.

Right before the benediction, she saw him squeeze into the back row. He really had come to see her! As soon as they were dismissed, she made as quick of a beeline as she could over to him. She decided that they were long past formalities after the previous day.

"Come with me." Isaac looked a little surprised at the lack of formalities, but she could see in his eyes that he was considering it.

"How long do I have to decide?" Her heart soared for a moment, but she reeled it back in. What if he said no?

"Three hours." She kept her voice as even as possible, but somehow a little tremor had found its way in. "Father is taking me to the Mennonite community so they can take me to the train station."

"Where are you going from there?" The fact that he was asking questions was making her nervous excited, but she wasn't sure if this was a good excited or if she would scare him off. She took a deep breath and told him of all the places she planned to visit with the money her parents had saved for her and what she planned to do with the money she had been saving. She told him of the research she had done on Rome, Paris, London, New York. Some of the information might have been a little outdated, she admitted to him, but she did the best she could to find the best prices for what she was trying to do.

Isaac was quiet for a few moments after she finished. The church had long been empty, but neither of them seemed to care.

"I think that sounds fun. I'll meet you at your house in a few hours." With that, he turned and started making his way out the door.

"Wait," he stopped at her words. "You're not still mad?" He smiled.

"Love doesn't keep record of wrongs. I already have your parents' blessing. What else is there to be mad about? You're a woman who knows what you want and how you want it. I may not be *exactly* what you were looking for, but I'm the best you're getting. And I'll blow all of your expectations of what a husband should be out of the water."

What happened next was a mystery to Sarah because suddenly she was in front of Isaac and they were kissing. But it wasn't just a kiss. This kiss awakened long-dead passion in Sarah that she didn't even know needed to awakened. She realized it wasn't that she didn't want to be married. It's that she didn't want everything to be fake. She knew then, kissing Isaac, that this was a real love that she wasn't going to get from anyone else in the whole world. And she loved him for it.

A REASON TO RUN : AN AMISH ROMANCE

DEIRDRA SCOTT

Chapter One

Leah Yoder breathed in the scent of fresh cut grass that floated in the air. Across the rolling acres of fields, her father and four brothers were working hard cutting hay.

Lifting a newly washed blue shirt up to hang on the clothes line, Leah smiled to herself as she listened to a pair of birds sing in a nearby field.

Fastening the shirt in place, Leah closed her eyes and soaked in her surroundings, drinking in the peace and harmony of the secluded farmland.

Reaching into her apron pocket, Leah felt for the letter that she had found in her mailbox early that morning. A secret note...from the most special person.

At twenty-one-years-old, Leah was one of the oldest unmarried women in her Amish community. For the longest time, Leah had worried that she might never find the perfect beau and that she might remain an old *madel* – old maid – forever.

But then Alvin Graber had moved to the area with his family. Leah had first spied him at church and felt instant attraction – and, *ach!,* what a pleasure it was to get to know him at the young peoples' singing. The two had quickly become friends and then their friendship had blossomed into romance.

"You look mighty happy to be hanging laundry!" The voice of Leah's sixteen-year-old sister Emma rang out, interrupting her thoughts.

Leah giggled and reached for another pair of wet pants.

"If chores make you this happy, maybe you should do mine as well," Emma suggested with a smirk.

Leah shook her head and exclaimed, "Come on, little sister! Look at this beautiful day...how could anyone not be happy? Laundry or not, it's still a great day to be alive."

Emma shook her head and rolled her eyes, "I have a feeling that you've got more to be happy about than the rest of us. You've managed to catch a pretty fine boyfriend and I'm figuring your happy smile might have something to do with him."

Leah tried to fight the blush that was starting to creep into her cheeks. Grabbing up a wet sock, she slapped at her younger sister.

"Are ya running off somewhere with him tonight?" Emma asked, obviously not finding the humor in her older sister's teasing.

Allowing her happiness to show on her face, Leah grinned from ear-to-ear and nodded, "He sent me a note this morning, inviting me on a late night buggy ride."

Emma obviously didn't share her sister's happiness. Letting out a grunt, she managed to announced, "Some of us aren't so lucky!"

Thinking back to her own days of being single, Leah couldn't help but feel a pang of sorrow for her little sister. Reaching out, she threw an arm around Emma's shoulder and announced, "Be patient, little sister, your day will come as well!"

Obviously, Leah's words didn't help since Emma only grunted in reply and then headed back into the house with an empty laundry basket.

But Leah wasn't going to let her little sister's sour attitude ruin her day – the afternoon was too perfect to let anything get her spirits down!

True to his word, Alvin arrived at the house with his buggy at seven o'clock that evening. Leah had sat on the porch waiting for him, reading a book as she enjoyed the peaceful sound of the crickets after a long day of chores.

Once she was up on the buggy seat beside her boyfriend, Leah soaked up the fun of the evening adventure, talking about everything that came to her mind as the horse clipped down the country roads.

"How was your day?" Leah finally asked, when she found a chance to catch her breath and slow down with her own chattering.

Alvin smirked and reached up to run a hand through his curly black hair, "I was wondering if I'd ever be able to get a word in around you," he teased.

Leah shook her head and ducked her eyes, embarrassed to realize that she had dominated the entire conversation.

"I'm just picking on ya," Alvin assured her as he gave her hand a gentle squeeze. Slowing the buggy, he took a deep breath and announced, "I wanted to meet up so that I could tell you the good news – today I signed papers on that farm I'd been looking at."

Leah felt her breath catch in her chest. Her brown eyes getting large, she studied her boyfriend in the darkness, almost worried that he was telling her a fib.

"*Ach*, are ya serious, Alvin? Is it really yours?"

A sly smile spread across Alvin's face as he pulled his buggy into an empty driveway and stopped the horses so that he could stare at her as he replied, "No, it's not mine, Leah. It's *ours*."

His words caused Leah's heart to feel like it would stop beating entirely. Her mouth dropped open and she felt at a total loss for words as Alvin continued, "Leah, I know we've only been dating since I moved here last winter, but I've always known you were the girl for me. I love ya, Leah. Would you do me the honor of becoming my wife and spending the rest of your life by my side?"

"Alvin..." Leah found herself so overwhelmed by emotion, she could hardly force words to come out of her mouth, "Oh, Alvin, yes! Oh, yes!"

Alvin's face broke out into a broad smile. Reaching out, he pulled he to him in a hug as he whispered, "There's a little abandoned trailer on the property – I can fix that up for us for now, if you don't mind living in such small spaces. And I'll start working on building us a new house immediately – something nice with lots of rooms where we can raise a couple dozen babies."

Leah had to laugh and whispered, "A couple dozen, eh?"

"A lot of good dishwashers and helpers on our farm," Alvin continued. Pulling back, he held her at arm's length and studied her face.

"Leah," he said softly, "You are sure, right?"

Reaching out in a playful manner, Leah grabbed his black felt hat off of his head and exclaimed, "I've never been more sure of anything in my life." Leaning forward, she kissed him.

The horse let out a noise and jerked slightly forward, knocking the hat right out of Leah's hand and sending it sprawling out into the deserted country road.

"Ugh!" Leah exclaimed, "How clumsy I am!"

"I think the horse is getting tired of waiting on us," Alvin returned with a laugh, "Don't worry about the hat – I'll get it."

But Leah was already scampering down from the buggy seat and hurrying onto the road. She was full of such excitement and energy, she felt like a little girl again.

Reaching down, she grabbed for the hat.

Suddenly, as if out of nowhere, headlights appeared. In a split second, Leah heard Alvin scream, "Watch out!", as the screeching of brakes filled her ears. Then everything went black.

Chapter Two

Leah struggled to open her eyes. Her eyelids felt so heavy – so impossible to lift. When she managed to force them open, she was met by the glow of bright, florescent lights shining above her.

Where was she?

Leah tried to remember what had happened. She tried to grasp for any clue of where she might be.

"*Mamm...*" She managed to mutter out a cry for her mother.

"I'm right here, sweet girl," The familiar voice of her mother filled her ears as Mrs. Yoder stepped up and put a reassuring hand on top of hers.

"We're both here," her dad replied as he stepped into view.

"Where am I?" Leah whispered, letting out a groan as a wave of pain overtook her.

"You're in the hospital," *Mamm* replied softly, "Leah, do you remember anything about last night?" Obviously noticing Leah's blank expression, she went on to explain, "Child, you were hit by a car. You were out with Alvin and he said that you jumped down to get his hat off the road when a car came out of nowhere and hit you head-on."

Now, memories came rushing back to Leah's mind. Suddenly, overwhelmed by the severity of the situation, Leah leaned back against her pillow, taking shaky breaths.

"Am I going to be okay?" She managed to whisper.

Reaching out to softly stoke her hair, *Mamm* nodded and forced a smile, "You're pretty beat up, but the doctors seem to be positive about everything."

Attempting to raise her arm, Leah winced as pain shot through her body.

"Try to lie still," *Daed* instructed, "You broke your arm and your leg."

Leah could certainly feel the pain in her arm but her leg...she couldn't feel anything at all there. Attempting to lift it, Leah was confused when she couldn't make it move.

"Are you sure my legs are still there?" Leah asked slowly, glancing at the foot of her bed in confusion, "I can't feel them at all."

Glancing from one parent to another, Leah insisted, "I can't feel my legs at all. Nothing. It's like they aren't there."

Leah's parents looked at each other, their faces suddenly becoming sober.

"What's wrong with me?" Leah asked, choking on a sob that threatened to overwhelm her, "*Mamm*...what's wrong with me?"

A rap on the door interrupted their conversation as a doctor poked his head into the room, "Hello," he called out as he made his way to

Leah's bedside, "I'm Dr. Barker and it is good to finally meet you while you're conscious, Miss Yoder."

Leah couldn't force herself to do more than offer a half-hearted smile. Taking a deep breath, she announced, "Doctor, something is wrong with me. I can't feel my legs at all. What's happened?"

Glancing at some of his charts, the doctor tried to sound cheerful as he announced, "You are one lucky young lady, Miss Yoder! You could have been killed in an accident like that. As it is, you have a broken arm, a shattered leg..."

"I can't feel my legs at all," Leah interrupted.

Taking a deep breath, the doctor continued, "Miss Yoder, when you were hit, your spine was seriously injured. Now that you're awake, we can do some tests and we can try to discover just how this might affect you in the long run..."

It seemed like the room was spinning around her. Leah felt like she might be sick to her stomach as she tried to soak in the doctor's words.

She was paralyzed.

He wouldn't say it, but she knew that it was true.

"How likely am I to ever walk again?" Leah interrupted him once more, no longer caring whether she was rude or not.

Dr. Barker shook his head slowly, "I can't tell you one way or another, Leah. It will just take time for us to get back the test results and get a grasp on the damage..."

"Do you think I will walk again?" Leah asked, "From what you've been able to tell, do you think I'll ever walk again?"

Dr. Barker was quiet for a moment, obviously struggling to determine how much he should tell her. Softly, he put a hand on top of hers and said, "I have known a lot of people who did amazing things that didn't have the use of their legs."

He continued to talk about women who had gone on to accomplish incredibly feats as paraplegics, but Leah was no longer listening. Closing her eyes, she tried to ignore everyone and everything.

She was a cripple.

She was ruined.

From the start, Leah had held out very little hope that things would get better – and that small ray of hope was quickly snuffed out by her test results. Dr. Barker finally had to amid that she would never walk again.

Leah's parents took turns staying by her side, trying to keep her spirits up but with no success at all.

There was nothing left for Leah.

One afternoon, Mr. and Mrs. Yoder had gone home to spend some time with their other children, leaving Leah alone.

Lying in her hospital bed, she stared dejectedly out the window, watching as cars whizzed by on the busy highway.

Leah felt completely exhausted, as if every ounce of strength had been totally drained from her body. Thinking back to life before her accident, Leah reached up to wipe a stray tear away from her eye.

There was a familiar rapping of knuckles against her hospital room door.

Leah realized that it was probably another doctor or nurse coming to poke and prod at her. Leaning back against her pillow, she shut her eyes, unable to find the energy to even answer them.

Slowly the door squealed open and she could hear the sound of boots making their way closer to her bed.

Opening an eye, she found Alvin standing at her side, an uncomfortable grin on his face and a package in his hands.

"Hello there!" He exclaimed, leaning over to give her a kiss on the top of her prayer *kapp*, "I wanted to come sooner, but your parents told me to wait." Pulling out a chair, he scooted over closer to her side and sat down, "I brought you a present."

He tried to hand the present to her, but Leah ignored him completely. Finally, giving up, he simply placed the package beside her on the bed.

"I have missed you so much, Leah!" Alvin exclaimed, "And I have been so worried about you! Do you have any idea when you get to go home?"

Leah gave a shrug and struggled to find her voice, "At this point, I really don't care."

Did Alvin know the truth about her? He surely didn't. There was no way that he would have come to see her if he knew that she was a cripple. There was no way that he would still care about her at all.

"Well, I care!" Alvin exclaimed, "We've got planning to do...we've got to get a plan drawn up for that house so I can go on and start building once I have some more money. We've got to figure out where you want to put the barn so it won't be too close to the house and yet it won't be so far that I have to trudged across miles of snow in the winter..."

Leah couldn't handle hearing his plans any longer. Throwing up a hand, she exclaimed, "Stop, Alvin! Just stop!"

"Haven't you heard about me?" Leah managed to ask, struggling to find her voice, "Haven't you heard what happened? Alvin...I'm a cripple now. The doctors say that I will never be able to walk again. I am broken and I am no good."

"Leah...I would never feel that way about you..." Reaching out, Alvin tried up put his hand on Leah's but she quickly jerked hers away.

"Just leave me alone, Alvin!" She exclaimed, her voice sounding harsher than she had hoped, "Just go away."

The sound of her parents entering the room relieved some of the stress.

Alvin pulled himself to his feet, obviously glad to have them there.

"Alvin!" *Daed* exclaimed, reaching out to pat him on the back, "It's so *gut* to see you here! I'm glad you were able to come today."

Feeling everyone turn to look at her, Leah crossed her arms defiantly against her chest, as if she could shield herself from the world.

"I've got to be getting home," Alvin announced, "I just wanted to bring a present by for Leah."

Looking her way, he said, "See ya later, Leah. Take care."

Leah didn't respond. She just turned her head to stare out the window.

Dad walked Alvin to the door. She could hear him muttering that things would "be better once they got home".

But things would never be better.

Leah was a cripple and there was no hope that life would ever again be good.

Chapter Three

Leah stared absent-mindedly out the window of the car as the driver pulled up to her house.

It was now September and Leah had spent her entire summer in the hospital and rehabilitation center. Looking at the trees in her front yard, Leah noticed that their green leaves had withered away to dry, crispy skeletons of their former beauty.

Just like me, Leah thought to herself.

At one point, Leah had been so hopeful for life – she was so full of energy and excitement, ready for whatever lay ahead. But now? Well, there was now nothing to look forward to. No hopes for the future. All she could see was a life of being taken care of by others...and then death.

"Let's get you inside," *Daed* announced as he pushed the car door open, letting in a breeze of cool air.

Leah let her father carry her to the house where *Mamm* hurried to set up her wheelchair inside the doorway.

Daed set her down carefully in her chair, obviously worried that he would hurt her in the process.

Leah felt awkward as Emma and her brothers gathered around staring at her. Although some of her siblings had come to see her while she was in the hospital, this felt a thousand times worse. In the hospital, she was expected to be sick and frail. Here at home, she should be whole and about herself.

Although she had known that things would never again be good, at least she had hoped that they would be better once she got home. Now, it seemed that things were only destined to be worse! As a wave of depression overtook her, Leah had to bite her lip to keep from crying.

"It's good to have you home, sister," Emma managed to say, although she sounded anything less than glad. She sounded so unsure of herself, so unlike Emma.

"We brought your bed downstairs," *Mamm* explained as she led Leah through the house and to a backroom which had once been a sitting room, "You *daed* and I thought that things might be easier this way."

Leah found herself gulping hard against a lump that was forming in her throat. Everything was different.

"I'm tired now." Leah announced, "I think I'd like to rest for a while now."

Leah saw her parents glance at each other as Dad hurried to ask, "Don't ya want to spend a little bit of time with the family? Maybe we could sit out on the porch and visit for a while."

Listening to her father try to act like things were normal was almost more than Leah could handle. Shaking her head, she announced, "No. I really am tired."

Finally nodding in agreement, her parents helped her into bed and then left her alone.

Alone.

Leah found tears streaming down her cheeks she realized that alone was all she had in her future.

The next day, Leah was sitting in her room, staring dismally out her window when *Mamm* announced that she had a visitor. Leah didn't even have to ask who it was.

Alvin.

He was back.

Just seeing him was almost too painful for Leah to bear. The sight of her old boyfriend reminded her of all the hopes and dreams of the past – hopes and dreams that were now shattered and left so far behind.

"It sure is *gut* to see you home!" Alvin exclaimed, making his way to sit in a rocking chair in her bedroom, "*Ach,* I've missed you so much, Leah."

Leah didn't respond. She didn't even look at him. She just stared out the window.

"Sunday's coming up soon and I'll be so glad not to be driving home from the young people's gathering by myself. That buggy seat gets mighty cold on these chilly fall nights when a guy's all alone."

"Then find another girl," Leah whispered.

"What did you say?"

"I said, find another girl." Leah raised her voice and turned so that she could stare her old sweetheart in the face, "Don't you see, Alvin? It's all over between us."

Alvin reached out and put a gentle hand on her shoulder, "Leah...you don't mean that. Sweetie, we've still a world of good things ahead of us!"

Leah jerked away from him.

He couldn't want her now. Not like this. She was completely broken. The only reason Alvin would ever want her was simply out of a feeling of duty and no longer of love.

"Leah, we've got a life to plan..."

"There is no life after this," Leah interrupted, growing almost hostile with frustration, "Alvin, you can't understand. I just wish that I'd died when that car hit me. If God truly loved me, He would have let me die. There's no use for a crippled Amish woman. I'm just going to be a nuisance for anyone who has to deal with me."

"Don't say such things!" Alvin exclaimed, "Leah, what are you talking about? I never loved you because you could walk! I love you because you are who you are. You are important to me. There is no other girl I would be happy with. Whether you can walk or not doesn't matter to me – I just want you in my life."

Leah didn't even want to hear him. No matter how nice his words were, Leah knew that they weren't true – they couldn't be true.

"Just leave, Alvin!" She finally announced, turning her wheelchair so that it no longer faced him, "Just leave me alone. I never want to see you again."

Alvin started to say something, he started to protest, but then he stopped himself. Leah listened as he let out a sigh and then turned to leave the room.

She was right. She knew that she was right. Alvin would be happier without her. She had nothing to offer him now.

Chapter Four

Leah skipped church that Sunday and chose to instead stay home alone. At first, her parents seemed nervous about leaving her alone, but they finally agreed. Leah was so relieved when they were gone.

Sitting alone in the silence of the house, she finally released all of her pent-up tears, sobbing aloud as they poured down her cheeks.

She was so hopeless now.

Leaning her head against her bed-frame, she cried until it felt like she could cry no longer.

"God…" Leah wanted to pray, but it was hard to make words even come out of her mouth. She felt so incredibly angry and betrayed.

"Why God?" She finally asked aloud into the stillness of the room, "Why did you let me live? What good is my life at this point? I'll never be anything but a burden to anyone! I'm just a problem. My parents will be stuck dealing with me until they die, and then Emma or one of the boys will have to take care of me. Why did you let this happen?"

Closing her eyes, Leah let the tears run down her face without even wiping at them. She wished so desperately for some kind of answers.

Reaching out for the Bible that *Mamm* had placed on her dresser, Leah opened it randomly.

Looking at the first verse her Bible landed on, Leah read, "Blessed is the man that trusteth in the Lord, and whose hope the Lord is."

How could she have hope now? What chance was there? Leah had always believed that God had a good plan for her life...that He was taking care of her, but now she was unsure of anything.

"Do you want me to be a cripple, God?" Leah asked into the stillness of her room, "Is this really what you want for me?"

It was the first time that she had ever consider that a possibility. Ever since the accident, she felt like God was punishing her, that He had turned His back on her. But what if she could still put her trust and hope in Him? What if, even when her legs were no longer working, He still had a purpose for her?

"God," Leah softened her voice, "I don't want to be in a wheelchair forever...but, if this is what you want for me, then so be it. Just please show me what I'm supposed to do next."

The prayer did not give her immediate comfort, but it gave her a sort of peace. It was in God's hands now – if He had some sort of plan for her life, then He was going to have to make it happen.

Monday morning Leah had an appointment at the hospital. Although her arm and leg had completely healed from their breaks, she still had regular follow-up appointments.

A friendly doctor examined her in the office room, asking questions about her condition.

"How are you doing on the inside?" Dr. Jane asked as she looked at Leah with a smile.

Leah felt her confidence fail her as she gave a shrug, "I don't know...I guess pretty lost still. I'm just praying and hoping that God still has some sort of plan for me in all of this. It seems like there isn't much point left in me living."

Dr. Jane nodded sympathetically and then announced, "Well, I certainly don't want to step out of place...but I think I might have something you can do while you're waiting to figure everything out." Motioning Leah to follow her, Dr. Jane led her out of the waiting room and through the hospital.

"I have someone that I want you to meet," Dr. Jane announced as she pointed Leah to a small hospital room.

Pushing her wheelchair along behind Dr. Jane, Leah followed her to a small incubator where a baby was lying. A nurse stood nearby, writing some information down on a chart.

"This poor little guy was born this morning," Dr. Jane announced, "He had some complications and they are keeping him because the doctors are afraid that he may have brain damage."

Reaching out softly, Leah placed her hand on top of the baby's head, stroking his hair.

"Where's the mom?" Leah managed to ask.

"She left right after he was born," Dr. Jane replied, "She just abandoned him here. We don't know if she didn't want him because of the brain damage or if she simply didn't want a baby. Right now, the hospital is teaming up with social services to locate a foster family or a relative who will take him."

Leah felt a lump growing in her throat as she thought about the poor little thing, completely abandoned by everyone.

"Poor little baby," she managed to whisper.

"Leah," Dr. Jane reached out to put a hand on her shoulder, "Every morning I come to this part of the nursery before my shift starts at the hospital and I rock babies. Some of them are like this little guy – totally abandoned. Others are sick because their parents have been on drugs and the babies have to go through a painful withdrawal. They have no one to hold them and no one to love them. I try to help them...but I can't hold them all. Would you be willing to consider becoming a volunteer? We could really use your help."

Looking at the baby, Leah nodded her head without even thinking. *Ach*, how could she say no to such an offer as that?

Obviously, God still had a plan for her. She had just been so caught up in her own pain that she was unwilling to open her eyes to the opportunities that she had to help others around her.

Reaching up to rub her eyes, Leah announced, "Of course. I would love to help."

Chapter Five

Once Leah began to realize that she could still help people, it felt like God started to open her eyes to a world of possibilities. Although her wheelchair confined her from running through the fields or taking long walks around the pond bank, it gave her a chance to do so many things she had never imagined tackling.

Not only did she start to volunteer to hold babies at the hospital, but she also began making rounds reading to children who were undergoing treatment for diseases and disorders.

"I'm starting to think my wheelchair is actually a blessing," Leah announced one night as she helped her *Mamm* dry dishes at the sink, "Today I met a little boy who is having surgery on his legs and is scared. I showed him that, even with a wheelchair, you can still be happy and enjoy life! Next, I want to start making presents for people in the local nursing home and maybe organize some activities for them. I think they would love it if some of the young folks in our Amish community would go sing for them at the retirement home! And I also want to send cards to people who are sick and having problems."

"Woah, girl!" *Daed* exclaimed, putting his hand up in surprise, "You've got so many plans, you're wearing me out!"

Leah had to grin at her father's statement.

"Not me!" Emma announced as she hurried to clear the table of the leftover meatloaf, green beans, fresh baked bread, and apple pie, "Leah's plans get me excited! I think I'd like to help her with some of these projects."

"I'd also like to make quilts for babies and children entering the foster care program," Leah let her ideas flow as quickly as they entered her mind, "And maybe I could make some quilts and sell them to help with that new homeless shelter they are starting in town."

"That was mighty good bread, Leah," *Mamm* announced, grabbing for another slice.

Leah had discovered that, even from her wheelchair, she could easily bake an entire meal with a little bit of help reaching items from a high shelf in the pantry.

"*Jah*, you are a mighty good cook!" Leah's little brother, Abram, announced, "I'm mighty glad that Alvin Graber is gone. I don't want you to leave us...ever!"

Although the little boy's words were sweet, they sent an instant pain through Leah's heart.

Alvin hadn't been back since the day that Leah turned him away. She tried to console herself by thinking about all the good that she was doing and the ways that God was using her to help others, but Leah couldn't erase the pain that attacked her sometimes.

Obviously, Alvin didn't love her. If he did, he never would have let her run him away.

Leah could feel her *daed* glancing in her direction.

"Boys, Emma," Dad closed the newspaper he had been reading and announced, "Why don't you go on and get ready for bed. Your mom and Leah can finish cleaning up."

Although they reluctantly left, the boys and Emma slowly exited the room, obviously wishing that they could stay behind to listen.

"Leah," *Mamm's* voice was gentle as she asked, "Have you talked to Alvin at all since he last came here to visit?"

Leah took a shaky breath as she put away the last of the silver-wear in a low drawer.

"No...I haven't. I've seen him at church, but he'll hardly look at me anymore." Shaking her head slowly, Leah announced, "I'm afraid I was right about him. I don't think that he wants to be with someone who is crippled."

"You hurt him, child," *Daed* informed her, "That boy was so worried about you while you were in the hospital."

"And you just pushed him away every time he tried to talk to you," *Mamm* added, her face growing serious, "Leah, how can you expect him to just keep hanging on forever?"

Leah could feel the darkness of depression start to cloud over her. Perhaps her parents were right – maybe she had destroyed her chances with Alvin, but surely it was for his best.

Forcing herself to go on with her work, Leah prayed silently to herself, asking God to do things in His own way and time. Perhaps it was the Lord's will that Leah never have a family of her own; maybe He wanted her to simply spend her life helping other people. If that was the truth, Leah would accept God's will.

Chapter Six

Leah was sitting on the front porch in her wheelchair filling out greeting cards and enjoying one of the last warm days of the fall when she spotted the buggy heading up the lane.

Raising her eyes, she watched the buggy travel closer and felt her heart skip a beat when she recognized the driver.

Alvin.

What was he doing coming to their home? It felt like her heart was in throat as he pulled his buggy to a stop in front of the porch and jumped down to the ground.

"Leah," Alvin called out, "Can ya talk for a minute?"

Leah found herself conflicted by so many uncertain feelings. She suddenly felt the same old awkwardness about her situation and began to wonder if Alvin was showing up simply to end their relationship for good.

"Sure," she managed to say, forcing a smile around her fears.

"Actually," Alvin put his boot up on the porch step, "I've got something I want to show you. Is there any chance you'd be willing to come with me?"

Leah gave a shrug and said, "That would actually be nice."

After putting her cards away in the house, Leah wheeled back out onto the porch.

"I'll have to have some help with this thing," she started to say.

"That's fine," Alvin assured her. Reaching out, he picked her up like a little child and carried her the short distance to his buggy. Once she was safely on the seat, Alvin folded up her wheelchair and put it in the back.

While the ride started out awkwardly, after a few minutes, Leah discovered that she was chatting as much as ever. She was so happy to tell Alvin everything about her new volunteer work and her plans to help others.

"Leah," Alvin pulled his buggy into a rugged driveway, carefully dodging a rough spot in the gravel, "We need to talk..."

Leah stared at him, wishing that she could open up her mouth and say all that was in her heart. She wanted so much to apologize, to let him know that she didn't mean to hurt him, but was afraid it would seem like she was trying to rekindle a romance he might no longer want to pursue.

Running his hand across his neck in frustration, Alvin said, "Well, let's not talk yet...let me just show you something."

Grabbing the reigns, Alvin told Leah to close her eyes and urged the buggy on up the lane.

Holding on tight to the buggy seat, Leah felt a smile cross her lips. Even if this was just a last visit, at least she would enjoy her bit of remaining time with this sweet friend of hers.

When Alvin pulled the buggy to a stop, he instructed Leah to keep her eyes closed as he helped her into her wheelchair and then pushed her a short distance.

"Open them, Leah," he finally instructed.

Leah opened her eyes and looked around her in confusion.

There was a house in front of her, but she wasn't sure who it belonged to or where she even was. Perhaps Alvin had brought her to visit relatives of his?

"Where am I even?" Leah asked with a laugh.

"When you were in the hospital, I worked harder than ever, Leah." Alvin explained, "This whole summer and fall, I have been struggling to get this finished...and it's almost done."

Noticing her confused expression, Alvin went on to say, "It's our place, Leah. This is the farm that I told you about and the house...well, I worked extra hours at my job and then built on this when I was off. My dad and brothers helped me get it this far along. We've still got some work before it's livable, but it's got a good start. By next spring, it will be ready."

Leah could hardly believe that Alvin had gone forward with his plans to build them a home. After she had spent so much time rejecting him and turning him away, Leah realized that he had never stopped loving her or holding onto hopes for their future together.

"Leah," Alvin got down on one knee beside her wheelchair and reached out to grasp her hand in his own, "I know that things are never going to be exactly like we'd planned, but that's life. When you need help, I'll be there to help you. And when I need help, you'll be there to help me. I need you in my life, Leah. Please...will you let me love you and be your husband?"

Leah felt like her heart was going to leap right out of her chest with joy. Alvin, dear, sweet man, truly did love her, regardless of her handicap. He wanted her in his life, and Leah wanted him in hers.

Reaching out, she pulled him to her in a hug and whispered, "Of course, Alvin. I am so sorry that it took me so long to come around. There is nothing in the world that would make me any happier!"

Leah didn't know what the future might bring. She wasn't sure what challenges were ahead of her, but she knew that with God and Alvin by her side, the future was looking bright.

LOVINA'S HEART

DEIDRA SCOTT

Chapter One

Lovina Miller took a deep breath as she reached up to pull a piece of laundry from the clothesline and put it in the basket at her feet. Above her head, a pair of bluebirds danced through the bright June sky, reminding her that summer was quickly approaching.

Summer. It was a time full of fresh starts and new beginnings.

Looking across the yard, Lovina watched David Yoder working with one of her brothers. Together, the two young men were struggling with their task, trying to break her *daed's* new horse.

Ach, just watching David sent a thrill of excitement through Lovina's heart. Although she had known him most of her life, there was something about him that could still put a spark inside of her, giving her the feeling that they had just met.

Growing up, Lovina had always dreamed of marrying David. It had just seemed natural to her. With their two houses located side-by-side, they had spent all of their childhood hours playing together in the creek that wound between their properties and climbing the big apple tree like little monkeys.

Lovina had decided early on that she and David would grow old together, spending their adult days raising babies and making a life within their Amish community.

Now that Lovina had turned eighteen-years-old, she felt like she was stuck in the midst of a waiting game, simply counting down the hours until David came forward to begin their relationship together.

Smiling to herself, Lovina basked in the realization that, as an adult, it was now time to watch her childhood dreams start to unfold.

"*Danki* for the help, David!" Lovina heard her father call out from the barn and looked up in time to see David waving goodbye to her family as he started across the yard.

Lovina felt her heart go aflutter when, rather than take the path back to his own parents' house, David veered closer to her own home and made a bee-line right for the clothesline where she was working.

"*Gut* afternoon, David!" Lovina called out, her voice seeming somewhat weak to her own ears.

Watching him come closer, Lovina couldn't help but marvel at how handsome her childhood friend had become. With a head-full of dark red hair and sparkling blue eyes, David had always looked like a cheerful storybook character; however, as he aged, he grew tall and muscular, his boyish looks transforming into that of a good-looking man.

"Hello there, Lovina," David called back, rolling down his sleeves as he walked along, "I tell you, that horse of your *daed's* nearly got me down this time!"

Lovina smiled as she pulled a pair of her brother's pants off of the laundry line and tossed them in the basket, "I guess we should consider ourselves glad to have such a good horse-breaker living so near-by."

To her surprise, David's face suddenly seemed to darken. Taking a deep breath, he reached up and put one hand on the clothesline, "Actually, Lovina, I wanted to talk to you about that."

Although Lovina had hoped that David would want to talk to her alone, she could already tell that his news wasn't going to be what she had wanted to hear.

"Lovina," David looked out across the fields, "Ever since you had your birthday, I'd been hoping..." his voice trailed off and he gave a shrug, "Well, nothing I'd hoped for is going to work out this summer." Standing up taller, he announced, "My uncle from Indiana wrote telling about the need for a good horse-trainer in his community. I agreed to go help for the next three months...I'll be home in time to help my dad get started on the harvest."

Lovina felt her heart drop in her chest. The idea that David would leave had never entered her mind. Even though it was only for three months, it felt like it might as well be three years.

"*Ach*, Lovina, don't be so sad," David reached out and placed his hand on her arm, "I'll be back – I promise. Kentucky is my home...I sure don't have any plans to run off for good."

Something about having his hand on her arm made the pain a little more bearable. Looking up, Lovina met David's tender gaze with her own.

"When I come back..." David took a deep breath and kicked at a clump of grass with his foot. It was strange to see him so uncomfortable – David was usually one to be bold and daring, willing to say whatever was necessary.

"When I come back, I hope we can spend more time together," David managed to say, "Seems like we've grown apart over the years, and I'm ready for that to end."

Lovina couldn't stop the smile that spread across her face, "And maybe not be climbing trees this time?" She added.

David laughed, "Of course we'll be climbing trees again!" He teased.

Growing more sober, he lifted his hand and ran it gently across her cheek, "I'll see you in three months, 'Vina."

Three months. As she watched him walk away and back to his parents' farm across the creek, Lovina took a deep breath and tried to still her thumping heart. Three months was a long time – she was just glad that she had those tender moments to cling to during the summer that stretched out before her.

Chapter Two

Taking a deep breath, David watched out the passenger window as the driver he had hired took him farther and farther from his home in Kentucky and on toward his Uncle Amos' house in Indiana.

"Are you nervous about leaving home for so long?" David's paid driver, Mr. Simpson asked, as he flipped his turn signal on and proceeded toward Uncle Amos' house.

David shook his head and laughed, "*Ach*, no, not nervous."

"Anxious to get away from your parents?" Mr. Simpson asked with a chuckle.

"No, nothing like that." David assured him, "Just glad to be helping my uncle and the people in his community."

Leaning his head back against the headrest of the seat, David closed his eyes and thought about Mr. Simpson's question.

Was he glad to be getting away from his parents? Although he had been quick to assure his driver that wasn't he case, David wasn't so certain himself. To be completely honest, David wasn't a bit sorry to be leaving for the summer. While he had always loved his home and his family, David relished the chance to get away.

Since David had been a little boy, he had always known what was expected of him. He was going to settle down, buy a piece of property close to his parents, and marry Lovina Miller. It wasn't a bad plan at all, but it seemed so boring and dull. Deep in his heart, David had always dreamed of excitement and adventure. Maybe his trip to Indiana would finally provide him with a chance to enjoy his freedom before he settled down for good.

David's driver took him straight to Uncle Amos' house, helped him unload his bags, and then left him to head back to Kentucky.

Uncle Amos and his entire family were happy to welcome David to their home. Uncle Amos explained that everyone in the community could use his horse breaking services and that they would be bringing their horses to his house so that David could train them. Uncle Amos also said that, during David's spare time he could help the family out in the dry goods store they had located in a small shed next to the road.

"I'll take you out to the store now, so that I can show you what kind of work you can do out there." Uncle Amos suggested once David had put his clothes away in the spare bedroom.

Leading David across the yard, Uncle Amos explained, "Of course, I will pay you for helping in the store...and you can also have all the money for training the horses."

David shook his head, "*Ach,* that's too much, Uncle Amos. I'm happy to have the chance to help out."

Uncle Amos chuckled and reached out to give David a slap on the back, "Now, now, don't go talking like that. I'm sure a handsome young man like you should be saving back to buy a nice farm and making plans for the future. I'd dare say that some pretty girl back home has caught your eye."

David gave a shrug, not too anxious to think about his future, "Nothing set in stone just yet."

The graveled lane ended and the two men found themselves standing side-by-side outside of the dry goods store. Reaching out, Uncle Amos pushed the door open, revealing a building with shelves full of baking supplies, canned goods, and some craft items.

"Hannah!" Uncle Amos called out, as he led David through the small building, "Hannah!"

"I'm over here," a soft voice returned.

Turning the corner around one of the shelves, they found a young Amish woman on her knees, busy stacking bags of flour.

"Hannah, I want you to meet my nephew, David," Uncle Amos announced, "David, this is Hannah – she is my wife's cousin and she's helping us out in the store this summer."

Hannah pulled herself to her feet and turned to stare up at David with large, blue eyes. Wisps of dark hair had escaped her prayer *kapp,* making a sort of halo around her face.

Just looking at her, David felt his heart give a leap. She was so unexpectedly beautiful in a dark, mysterious way.

"*Gut* to meet you, David," Hannah replied timidly.

"David is likely to be helping out in the store when he isn't working with the horses," Uncle Amos explained. Giving David a pat on the arm, he motioned toward the back room, "Come on, I want to show you where I store the bulk supplies."

As David followed his uncle, he had a hard time even listening to what was being said. His mind was still mesmerized by the beautiful and timid young lady he had just met. David could hardly wait to get to know and learn more about Hannah.

Lovina sat on the edge of her bed, looking out across the fields of farmland through her bedroom window. Knowing that David was no longer in the house next-door left a hollow emptiness in Lovina's heart. In her eighteen-years, she had never gone a summer without seeing David.

Lovina tired to imagine what her sweet friend was doing at that moment. Did he realize how much she was thinking of him? Did he miss her at all?

Lovina closed her eyes and took a deep breath, "Dear God," she whispered into the darkness, "Please, bring the man that I love back to me."

Chapter Three

David carefully guided his uncle's buggy down the road. It was only his second day in Indiana and work was already starting to pick up; however, Uncle Amos had sent him to town to pick up some nails for a woodworking project he was doing in the barn.

The summer afternoon sun shone down on David and the warmth of the breeze put a smile on his face. David was enjoying his time away from home and, although he had not had many opportunities to spend time with Hannah, he had hopes that would change eventually.

The buggy suddenly took a lung, pulling David out of his thoughts.

"Woah, boy! Woah!" David pulled tightly on the reigns, unsure of what was happening to the buggy. Carefully guiding the horse to the side of the road, he jumped down from his seat and looked over the situation.

Something was wrong with the front buggy wheel. Grabbing a hold of it, David gave it a wiggle, trying to determine if it could keep going.

Pulling off his straw hat, David slapped it against his leg in frustration. He couldn't get to town on that wheel and he didn't think he could make it back to his uncle's house either.

The clipping of oncoming horse hooves made David stand up straighter and wave desperately at the approaching buggy.

The driver was a single Amish man. As soon as David caught his attention, the other driver pulled his buggy to the side of the road behind David.

"Hi there!" David greeted with a smile as he watched the other Amish man get off his buggy and start toward him, "Boy, I sure am glad to see you!" Sticking out a hand, he announced, "I'm David Yoder. I'm staying with my Uncle Amos Yoder – you probably know him."

The stranger nodded and simply said, "I'm Luke Christner." Taking a deep breath, he walked over to the buggy and squatted down to inspect the wheel.

"Looks like this is busted good," he announced, pushing his hat back on his head and reaching up to wipe some sweat from his brow.

David groaned, "I was afraid of that."

Standing to his feet, Luke continued, "I'm afraid you shouldn't drive it any farther than just a few feet or you'll end up wrecking or destroying your entire buggy." With a slight smirk, Luke added, "Lucky for you, this is my parents' drive right up ahead. And I just happen to work on buggies for a living."

David's eyes got large and he let out a huge sigh, "Oh, *gut*! Do you think that you could help me out?"

Luke nodded, "Sure thing. Just lead your buggy down to my workshop. I'll have her fixed up in just a bit."

True to his word, Luke had the buggy wheel fixed within an hour.

David stayed by the young man who had rescued him and worked to fill him in on all the details about his life, his home, and his family. Luke, who seemed to be more reserved, was happy to listen and donate very few details of his own.

"How much do I owe you?" David asked as Luke put the repaired wheel back on his buggy.

Luke gave a shrug as he secured the wheel in place, "Nothing. Consider it a welcome present. Maybe you can help me with one of my horses one day this summer."

"*Ach*," David raised an eyebrow, "I can't let you do that. I took some time you could have been working on other projects..."

Before he could finished, Luke started shaking his head, "No, no you didn't," he assured David as he stood up straight, "Honestly, I didn't have any other work for today." Sighing deeply, he announced, "As badly as we need a horse trainer in this area, we do not need any kind of buggy work. Jobs around here are scarce, David. I was glad to help."

David pondered Luke's statement for a moment. As an idea entered his mind, a broad smile spread across his face, "Listen, Luke! You may not be needed here, but you sure would be in my community! How would you feel about going to Kentucky to spend the summer with my family? It would sure help them out while I'm gone, and you could earn money doing buggy repairs and carpentry work!"

Luke was silent, obviously studying David's suggestion. Finally, with a shrug, he announced, "*Jah* – I don't see why that wouldn't be great. *Danki*, David."

The entire plan made David's face light up like that of a little boy. Grinning from ear-to-ear, he grabbed his new friend's hand in a shake and started making plans to get Luke back to Kentucky.

Chapter Four

Lovina reached up to wipe some sweat from her forehead as she took a break from chopping weeds out of the row of green beans. Despite all her hard work, the weeds were quickly starting to overtake the plants.

David had now been gone two weeks, and Lovina had yet to hear anything from him. His absence made her sad and she wished for all she was worth that she would receive a letter.

Glancing across the field toward his house, she thought of all the times they had snuck away from their chores and played together instead.

To her surprise, Lovina saw a young man approaching her. Could it be…? Lovina's heart dropped as he drew closer. Although she had hoped that it was David, she instantly realized that her eyes had been playing tricks on her. This stranger was even taller than her dear childhood friend and slightly thinner.

"Hullo," Lovina called out as he continued to draw closer.

"Hullo," the stranger returned, his voice deep and almost mysterious, "Are you Lovina Miller?"

Lovina stood up straighter and adjusted her prayer *kapp*, "That would be me. Do I know you?"

The stranger shook his head, "No, you don't." Now he was so close that Lovina was able to get a good look at him. This strange Amish man looked to be in his early twenties, but he seemed more mature. His brown hair was so dark it was almost black, and his eyes a dark color chocolate. Just looking at him made Lovina take a deep breath of surprise. *Ach*, it was hard to remember a time that she had ever seen such a *gut*-looking man!

"I'm Luke Christner. I know your friend, David, and I'm staying with his family until he returns." Glancing toward her house, Luke asked, "Is your *daed* at home? The Yoders told me that he has a construction crew and I'd like a job."

Lovina felt so out of sorts, she wasn't sure what to do. Looking down at her bare feet, she tried to gather her composure. Taking a deep breath, she said, "*Nee*, my *daed* isn't home from work yet, but we're expecting him any minute. If you'd like to wait in the house, my *mamm* can give you some fresh lemonade and cookies."

Luke glanced from the house back to Lovina and then shrugged, "If you don't mind, I'll just stay out here. Looks like you could use some help." Grabbing for an extra hoe, Luke set to work, removing the pesky weeds from among the rows of bean plants.

There was something about Luke that made Lovina feel uncertain about everything. He was a good help in the garden, but she certainly would have felt more at-ease without him. On the other hand, she dreaded him leaving once her father got home from work. Just being near him made her feel things that she had never experienced – she found herself overwhelmed by a sort of giddiness that sprung up from deep within. Although Lovina had always been a talker, she suddenly seemed almost speechless.

"You don't have to do this," Lovina assured him.

Luke simply set his jaw and turned to look at her with his brooding, dark eyes, "I don't have to...but I want to."

Lovina felt weak in the knees, as if she might keel right over. Taking a deep breath, she tried to stead herself.

Suddenly, she found herself a little glad that David was going to be gone for the summer. As quickly as the thought flitted through her mind, she pushed it away; however, just the realization that she could think such a thing left Lovina questioning everything about the future.

David washed his hands in a pail of water that had been set out by the barn, preparing himself for the evening meal. Inside the house, Aunt Miriam was putting the finishing touches on a pot of homemade chili with the help of three of David's cousins.

True to Uncle Amos' word, in the time that David had spent in Indiana he had already been so busy, he hardly had time to even think about being at home.

Wiping his clean hands on a towel, David glanced across the acres of land that his uncle owned. There, in the glowing darkness of the evening, he could make out the form of a young woman walking near the pond.

Hannah.

David had learned to recognize her from a distance. Even though it would be hard to distinguish her from any other Amish woman from so far away, David could pick Hannah out because she was always alone. It seemed like she carried an air of sadness with her, wherever she went.

Taking a deep breath, David stepped out of the barn and started the short walk to the pond.

"Hi there," David called out as he drew near to Hannah.

The young woman looked up at him and gave a sad smile.

"What are you doing?"

Hannah gave a shrug and pulled her black shawl tighter against her shoulders, "I just felt like a walk," she explained.

David stepped up next to her side, "It must be sort of lonely to walk all alone."

Hannah shrugged again, "I'm used to being alone."

David *thought* over his childhood and how little time he had ever spent just to himself. There were always siblings to play with, other Amish children to enjoy at events, and Lovina. Lovina had always been there for him.

Just the thought of his old friend's name sent a nagging sense of guilt through his mind.

Hadn't he promised Lovina that, when he got home, things would be different? Hadn't he promised that they would spend time together? So, what was he doing, trying to get closer to Hannah?

"David..." Hannah's soft voice brought him out of his thoughts, "Are you all right, David? I've never seen you so solemn and quiet."

David looked up at her in surprise, his face breaking out in a broad grin, "Oh, *jah*, I'm fine. I was just thinking is all."

"I didn't know you were able to do that...you know, think without saying what was going through your mind." Although Hannah's words were haughty, David *looked* up in time to catch a teasing smile cross her lips. It was the first time he had ever seen her smile and, something about it made him want to see it a thousand times more.

"Maybe it's too much time around you," David suggested, "Because I don't think you ever say anything much at all."

Hannah's tender smirk turned into a broad smile and David was, once again, captivated by her charm.

Reaching out, he gently took her elbow in his hand, "Would you do me the honor of letting me walk with ya tonight?"

Hannah was silent for a moment, studying David for all that he was worth. Finally, she nodded slowly and said, "*Jah* – I suppose that might be nice."

Chapter Five

Just as David had predicted, it was easy for Luke to find work in Kentucky. He not only spent his afternoons working on buggies in the Yoder's empty shed, but also joined the carpentry work crew lead by Lovina's father.

Lovina wasn't exactly sure how it happened, but it seemed that she and Luke were constantly thrown in the paths of one another. Lovina tried to convince herself that it was merely a coincidence, but she had to admit that it was more than that.

The longer David was gone, the less she was thinking about him and the more she was thinking about Luke.

When he wasn't busy with work, Luke frequently dropped by to help Lovina in the garden; although he wasn't a talker, there was something about his calm attitude that left Lovina yearning for more time with him.

One evening, Lovina baked a plate of her famous homemade ginger snap cookies and decided to take a few across the creek as a thank you for Luke's help in the garden.

Knocking on the shed door, she cautiously pushed it open, cheerfully announcing, "Hello! Luke! Are ya in here?"

"*Jah*, I'm here," Luke replied.

There he was, standing next to a work bench with a busted buggy wheel laid out in front of him.

"Hi there!" Lovina greeted him, suddenly feeling unsure of herself and terribly bashful, "I thought I might bring you something." Placing the plate of cookies on the work table, she watched Luke eyeball them before picking one up and putting it in his mouth.

"It's just a thank you for all the help you've been giving me," she explained.

Luke raised his eyebrows and nodded as he swallowed, "*Danki* – they're very good. You're a good baker, Lovina."

Lovina felt her heart skip a beat with his compliment. Looking at the work he was doing, she added, "Looks like you've got quite a few talents of your own."

Reaching for another cookie, Luke gave a shrug, "I keep busy for sure....but that's a good thing. I'm always thankful for the money."

Leaning back against the table, Lovina studied him in the growing darkness, "Saving back for a farm of your own?"

Luke stared straight at his work and shook his head, "No. I'm going to give my money to help out my family. I have no need of a place of my own."

"Don't you ever hope to get married and have a family?"

Luke shook his head slowly, "I'm afraid all of my dreams are gone. I plan to be alone forever."

His words broke Lovina's heart. Although he tried to sound resolved, it was easy to hear the pain in his voice.

"*Ach*, Luke," she managed to whisper with a smile, "Don't say that. You never know what might happen."

Luke took in a deep breath and then let it out slowly. Looking up to meet Lovina's eyes, he studied her for what seemed minutes before asking, "What about you? Do you think that you could ever love someone like me?"

His question took Lovina by such surprise that she almost fell over. Her eyes growing large, she looked down at the floor, her heart flooded by a million different emotions.

"I...I...Luke..." Lovina's voice was trailing in every direction but her words were making no sense at all.

"Lovina," Reaching out, Luke put his hand on top of hers, "Would you consider going with me to the singing after church this weekend?"

It felt like Lovina would not be able to breath, so many decisions were running helter-skelter through her mind. Almost a surprise to herself, she heard her voice say, "Sure. I don't see why not."

Although David had been staying busy with the horses, he still managed to make some time to help out in the store. With a beautiful girl like Hannah there, he had to find time to spend with her.

One afternoon they had received a large order of supplies and were hurrying to put them on the shelves before it would be too dark to see, even by the glow of the lantern.

"*Ach*, this is a job!" David grumbled as he hurried to put some bags of flour in their place on a shelf, "Of course this would just happen to be the night that Uncle Amos and his entire family went visiting...leaving you and me to do all the work."

Hannah smiled and shook her head, "David, you complain so much. I don't mind the work. Work keeps me busy...work keeps my mind off of...other things."

Suddenly interested, David looked up in surprise. Maybe he would finally have a chance to hear some of the secrets that were hidden away behind this mysterious girl's sad blue eyes.

"What other things?" David asked.

Hannah shrugged as she ran her fingers over a bag of sugar, "Disappointments...heartbreaks...bad decisions."

Hannah went silent, assuring David that he would hear no more of her story, but then she surprised him when she went on to clear her throat and say, "I had a boyfriend...a fiancé even."

As the words came pouring out of her mouth, it was easy to see that they were tearing her apart. Hannah closed her eyes and continued, "But things didn't work out. We were engaged but...well, I was filled with so many uncertainties. I called off the wedding before it was even announced in church. I didn't mean to end everything with him – I just needed more time to think. But I'm afraid he took it as an outright rejection. And now, I'll never have a chance with him again," Hannah reached up to wipe away the tears that were threatening to overwhelm her, "*Ach*, David, it almost breaks my heart to talk about it. I have destroyed all my chances for happiness."

Looking at her in the light of the lantern, her face clouded over with pain and tears gathering in her eyes, David felt totally broken for her. Pulling himself to his feet, he stood up straight and stepped closer to her, putting a hand on her thin shoulder.

"Hannah," he whispered her name with all the tenderness that he had been storing in his heart, "Dear Hannah...you still have a thousand chances for happiness." Reaching up, he took his thumb and brushed a tear off of her cheek.

Hannah took a deep breath and let it out slowly. Looking at him in surprise, she simply whispered, "*Danki*, David." Then she squared her shoulders and announced, "Let's get back to work."

Chapter Six

Over the next few days, David and Hannah had little time to spend together. He looked forward to ever chance he had to see her. Although their friendship had not had time to progress, David felt confident that over the rest of the summer he could easily earn himself a special place in Hannah's lonely heart.

One afternoon, David had finally found a chance to work in the dry goods store alongside Hannah when one of his cousins came rushing into the shed with a letter in his outstretched hand.

"David," the little cousin called out, "You got some mail!"

Taking the letter, David quickly recognized the handwriting as that of his younger sister, Lydia.

Ripping the seal open, David pulled out the letter, unsure why his teenage sister would even take the time to write him.

Dear David,

I don't want to bother you while you're gone, but I need to let you know something important. I've always thought that you and Lovina had something special together, although I'm not sure if you had any kind of plans for the future or an agreement. While you've been gone, Lovina has taken a spark to the very man you sent here to work – Luke Christner. Seems like they're seeing each other almost every day and last night I overheard him invite her to the singing Sunday night. She agreed to go with him.

I don't mean to stick my nose in where it doesn't belong, but I know that you were always sweet on Lovina and just thought you should know.

Your sister,

Lydia

"*Ach*," David read over the letter and then reread it again, his heart suddenly dropping into his stomach.

Lovina – with Luke? A multitude of emotions suddenly assailed David. He found himself so frustrated, almost angry at Luke for stealing his girl. How dare Luke go to David's own home and try to take the woman he loved away from him? David was hurt, so hurt, by Lovina's decision to move forward with a relationship with someone else. But, worst of all, David felt incredible guilt and sadness.

Deep in his heart, David realized that it was his own fault that Lovina and Luke were growing close. In all the time that David had been in Indiana, he had never taken the time to even write his childhood sweetheart a letter – he had just always taken for granted that she would be there for him when he returned.

While he had been busy pursing a friendship with Hannah, he had never thought that Lovina might be looking at someone else.

Reaching up, David rubbed his hand across his face, trying to gather his wits and decide what to do next.

"What is wrong, David?" Hannah asked softly as she stepped up next to him.

David balled his free hand up into a fist, fighting the urge to destroy the letter he had just received. Passing it to Hannah, he quickly explained, "I don't know how to tell you this, Hannah, but Lovina...well, she and I have always been friends. I don't mean to have led you astray in any way because I have liked you since the day we met but this..." David couldn't go on.

Hannah took the letter in her own hands and read it slowly, her eyes growing large as she went over the message again and again.

"David," she managed to breath softly, "What are you going to do?"

David brushed his hand through his hair as memories of Lovina ran across his mind, "I don't know. I just don't know." Turning, he gave the floor a hard kick with the toe of his boot.

"David," Hannah took a deep breath and shook her head slowly, "I hate to say this, but you know that we aren't meant to be together. No matter how happy we might have both been to pretend...it just isn't so. You have made my summer much more enjoyable...but it's time to get back to our real lives."

David looked down at his feet. He wanted to fight her words; he hated the idea of giving Hannah up completely. But, when he thought of his dear Lovina...he knew that he couldn't live without her.

"Go to her, David!" Hannah exclaimed, "Go to Lovina and let her know that you love her."

Taking a deep breath, David nodded his head, "I'll go call a driver right now."

Chapter Seven

David sat in the passenger seat of the truck, half-heartedly listening as his driver talked incessantly during the long trip back home. Looking out the window, David watched the scenery slowly change from the flat Amish country of Indiana to the rolling hills of Kentucky.

With each mile that passed, it seemed that David got even more nervous about his future with Lovina.

When he first started home, he had been certain that she would be glad to see him but now...well, the closer he got to her, the less sure he became. Maybe she had truly fallen for Luke and she wouldn't want to even see him. Maybe David had blown his one and only chance for true love with the only girl he ever truly cared for.

Lovina had just filled up a bucket of water and got down on her knees to scrub the kitchen floor with a scrub brush when she heard a truck pull up in the front yard.

Ach, Lovina thought to herself as she plunged her hands down into the soapy water, *Daed must have visitors.*

It was Saturday afternoon and Lovina found her mind plagued with thoughts of Luke and their upcoming date. Although she truly enjoyed spending time with him, there was something about agreeing to go on a date with him that put her mind entirely in a tizzy. As much as she liked Luke and was attracted to him, Lovina battled thoughts of David – it seemed so sad to be turning her back on their relationship with each other.

But, she reasoned to herself, when she thought back on it, she and David had never had a true relationship. Sure, he had always been a good friend to her, but it seemed that was all things were to ever be. Since he left for Indiana, she had not heard a word from him and, as sad as she was to admit it, she was starting to wonder if he would ever come home at all.

"Lovina."

The voice seemed to come out of no where. Lovina looked up in surprise, wondering if she was truly hearing a person or if it was her own imagination.

There, standing in the doorway to the kitchen, was David himself.

"David!" Lovina managed to breathe as she struggled to pull herself to her feet, "Oh, David...is that really you?"

In an instant, David had bridged the space between them. He came right to her side, nearly knocking her bucket of soapy water over in his hurry.

"Lovina," David managed to say, somewhat louder this time, "Lovina..." he seemed to want to say more, but acted as if he couldn't find the words. Reaching out, he grabbed Lovina and gathered her into his arms.

To Lovina, everything felt like a crazy dream. Pressed firmly against her old friend's body, all thoughts of Luke vanished from her mind as she let David hold her like a little girl.

"Lovina," David pulled back only long enough to kiss her on the mouth, "Lovina, I have been a total moron. I am so sorry!"

"David," Lovina managed to say as she tried to catch her breath, "David...what has happened?"

David stepped back as he struggled to gather his composure. Reaching up, he wiped away at tears that threatened to overtake him.

"Lovina," he reached out and held her hands in his own, "I have been so ignorant. I left home, anxious to find adventure and experience new things...and I almost lost the one thing that means the most to me in the world – you."

Lovina felt her heart start to melt as David poured out his soul to her, "Lovina, I love you. I love you more than I ever realized. I thought that Uncle Amos was giving me a chance to experience adventure but I think it was actually the good Lord allowing me the opportunity to realize how much I love you. Please, Lovina...I don't want to wait any longer. Say that you will marry me!"

There had never been anything that Lovina wanted more. In that instant, it felt like all of her hopes and dreams were finally coming true.

Luke.

The name entered her mind suddenly and it felt like the life was drained right out of her. Oh, but hadn't she already led him to believe that she cared for him? Hadn't she already agreed to go out on a date with him this very weekend?

"David," Lovina squeezed her dear friend's hands tightly as she looked for the right words to share her news, "David. I have been a foolish girl."

"And I have been a foolish man," David was quick to add.

Lovina smiled and shook her head, "Perhaps we've both been foolish..."

Her words were cut short as the sound of an approaching vehicle brought them both from their thoughts.

Glancing out the window, they watched together as a strange car stopped in front of the house and let out a passenger.

David felt his heart sink when he saw the visitor who was getting out of the strange car.

It was Hannah.

David thought that she had understood. What was she doing...following him all the way to Kentucky of all places? Hadn't she been the one who had said that their relationship wasn't going to work and even pushed him to return to Lovina? What was she doing here now?

David battled the urge to run forward and stop her before she could get to the house. Turning to Lovina, he struggled to find the words to explain what was surely about to come.

"Lovina..." he hurried to say, "While I was gone, I was an idiot. I hate telling you this more than you will ever know, but I got involved with a girl from Indiana. We never started to court, but we were heading in that direction when I heard that you and Luke had begun a relationship...."

As the words poured from his mouth, David watched Lovina's face turn ashen and then red with shame.

"You already know about Luke?" She managed to whisper.

David nodded his head, "That was the wake-up call I needed. That was what I needed to bring me back home. I never want to risk losing you again, Lovina!"

Lovina started to wipe tears away from her eyes, "David, I don't want to lose you either! But what you heard is true. Luke and I have grown close and are on the verge of starting a relationship. I was so foolish, David, but I was afraid I had lost you and now I don't know what to do…"

In the other room, they could hear a knock on the front door.

Wiping at her eyes, Lovina hurried to go open it with David trailing close behind. When she opened the door, Hannah was standing on the front porch, a determined look in her blue eyes.

"I need to talk to David," she announced, looking from Lovina to David.

"David," she took a deep breath, "I need to go to your house…I need to see Luke."

Luke? David was more confused than ever. Cocking his head to one side, he tried to understand where this strange twist came into play.

"You don't have to look far," the deep voice of Luke spoke out and they all turned in surprise to find that he had come up on the porch and was standing just out of view.

"Hannah," as he said the name, his voice seemed to fill with a strange sort of pain.

"*Ach*, Luke…" Hannah looked down at her black shoes as if she couldn't hold his gaze, "I have been wanting to talk to you."

Luke shook his head sadly, "I can't imagine what we would have to say to each other now."

"Luke…you know that I am a very shy girl," Hannah said in a shaky voice, "And I have let my fear get the better of me far too many times. I almost let it destroy what we had together. But Luke…I can't let that happen."

David's eyes got large as he realized that Luke must be the ex-beau that Hannah had told him about.

"I love you, Luke," Hannah announced resolutely, "I love you and I still want to be your wife...if you can ever find it in your heart to have me."

David watched Luke and held his breath, hoping that he would agree.

Stepping forward, Luke reached out and took Hannah in his arms, "I love you too, Hannah!" He exclaimed as he cupped her face in his hands, "I have always loved you and I always will." Turning to look at Lovina, he quickly tried to explain, "Lovina, I hope that you understand..."

Lovina smiled broadly as she wrapped her arms around David's waist, "It is fine, Luke. I think that things are exactly the way that they are supposed to be!"

Epilogue

Standing together at the kitchen sink, Lovina and David watched as a group of children played outside in their front yard.

"Look at those crazy things," Lovina muttered as she noticed her daughter trying to climb a tree.

"Just like us when we were little," David announced.

Lovina looked up at him and smirked, "*Jah* – and I think our little girl might have a crush on the neighbor boy, as well."

David and Lovina had now been married for ten years and had three children of their own. It had been a double wedding shared with Hannah and Luke, who decided to move to Kentucky so that Luke would continue to enjoy a steady stream of work.

David and Lovina had built their house behind his parents' place and, to their surprise, Hannah and Luke had bought a piece of farm land right across the creek.

Their children played together and it wouldn't be any surprise if someday those same children would grow up to marry one another.

David smiled broadly and gathered his wife up in his arms.

"I'm glad I went to Indiana that summer," he announced as he reached out to push a strand of her brown hair back from her face, "Because that summer showed me how much I need you in my life."

Bending over, he gave her a gentle kiss.

Life truly was as David and Lovina had always imagined it – and they were happier than they ever could have guessed possible.

THE END

THE AMISH TEACHER

MONICA MARKS

Amish School Teacher

Jacob

Jacob shivered and adjusted the coat around his ears, his breath escaping his mouth in streams against the frigid Wisconsin air.

The snow was packed solid against the fields and the twelve-year-old stuffed his mitted hand into the depth of his trousers, silently warding off the cold.

It seemed that each winter was worse than the last and began earlier.

It is only early December, he thought with woe. *What will January and February hold?*

The one room school house was just ahead and he thanked *Gotte* for small favors; he was sure his toes would freeze clear off in his boots if he had to walk much further.

"Jacob!" someone called, causing him to pause.

He turned, using a wool mitten to brush a stray curl from his forehead and watched as Emma King slid toward him on mutton boots. Jacob noticed that her cheeks were likely as crimson as his from the ice in the atmosphere.

It gave him a small comfort to know someone else was with him in his plight but Emma often was his partner in most situations. They had grown up together in their district and lived only two farms apart.

She was breathless as she tried to catch up to him and Jacob waited impatiently.

"Hurry up, Emma," he growled at her gruffly. "I will freeze on the spot if I must stand here waiting."

Emma tried to move more quickly but her foot slipped against a fresh patch of ice and she fell unceremoniously into a pile of long brown skirts and cloak two feet from Jacob.

He hurried toward her, extending is hand to help her on her feet and she rose in a gasping laugh.

"You should not have rushed me, Jacob," she chided jokingly. He chuckled also, watching as she brushed the snow from her dark cloak.

"We best hurry, Jacob. Ingrid had already scolded me about being late once this week."

"Why are you always late?" Jacob asked as they turned back to make their way up the shoveled pathway to the building.

The others had already gone inside, escaping the bitter cold to warm their hands by the wood stove.

"No reason," Emma replied, glancing at him out of the corner of her eye. He glanced at her expertly pressed braids and idly wondered who had done them so prettily.

"Emma King, this is the second time - oh, Jacob! You have arrived also!"

Their school teacher, Ingrid abruptly stopped her lecture of Emma to smile sweetly at the young man with the tardy girl.

"Why are you smiling at him and scolding me?" Emma asked sullenly. Ingrid's rosebud mouth formed a small line and her blue-grey eyes narrowed with annoyance.

"Perhaps because you have no respect for your elders and you are consistently late. You can begin by writing out today's math lesson on the board."

"But I am frozen! My hands will not cooperate with the chalk! "Emma protested.

"You will not argue with me, Emma!" Ingrid snapped and Jacob nudged his friend.

"Emma, do as you are told," he murmured. Emma scowled slightly and turned away, unfastening her cloak as she moved further into the coatroom.

"How are you, Jacob?" Ingrid asked as Jacob removed his wet boots, droplets of water falling to the floor.

Jacob glanced at her, his dark eyebrow raising slightly.

"I am just as well as I was yesterday at worship," he replied in confusion.

"And how are your siblings? Are they well also?"

Jacob nodded slowly, his pulse quickening.

"Why do you ask?"

"Oh, no reason," Ingrid replied quickly. "I was merely making conversation. Come inside and warm yourself before sitting."

The young schoolmarm turned away, leaving Jacob to stare after her.

He had noticed that she had been paying special attention to him in the past months and it made him nervous.

Is there something she knows which I do not? He wondered.

Ingrid always asked about his family and his health.

Is someone in my family ill? Are there rumors circulating which I know nothing about?

Dozens of terrifying thoughts ran through his mind but he could not read anything but pleasant attentiveness on Ingrid's face.

Jacob was not accustomed to people noticing his presence.

His family was in good standing in the district. Like so many other Amish families in Cashton, they were dairy farmers, supplying the local cheese factory with milk.

They were a large family, the Wyses, seven siblings in total, Jacob the third youngest and often lost in the middle of the herd.

Not that anyone else is much more descript than me in the family, he thought dryly as he took his spot at a scarred desk near the front of the room.

The Wyse family was well known for their meek dispositions.

Jacob was possibly the most outspoken of the gaggle but even so, he preferred to sit in the background just like his brothers and sisters.

And as the day progressed, Jacob found an anxiety growing in his bones as Ingrid continued to offer him small beams.

Why does she look at me like that? He wondered.

By day's end, Jacob had decided that he needed to ask her and waited for the others to leave the small house.

"Jacob, will you walk home with me?" Emma called to him from the entranceway but he shook his head.

"No," he replied. "I need to see Ingrid."

"Oh. All right."

He didn't notice the disappointment on her face as she exited.

"What do you need to see me about, Jacob?" Ingrid asked, coming from the coat room. She had apparently heard his words and her pale brow creased in confusion.

"You have been staring at me all day. Why?"

Ingrid's face turned scarlet and she shook her head in denial.

"I have not!" she declared hotly. Jacob was suddenly uncertain.

"Oh...are you sure? I feel like you continue to watch me as if you know some terrible secret about me."

Ingrid laughed and shook her long, blonde hair.

"Of course not, Jacob. I am sorry if I made you feel uncomfortable. I was just..."

He stared at her expectantly but she did not finish her thought.

"No," she said instead. "I have not been staring at you. Perhaps I must pay more attention to where I am looking from now onward."

Jacob was suddenly very embarrassed and he lowered his head.

"My apologies," he muttered.

"It's all right, Jacob."

She turned away from him to wipe the blackboards clean but as Jacob shuffled away to leave, Ingrid's voice piped up again.

"Uh, Jacob," she said haltingly. He paused to look back at her.

"Yes?"

"Tell Samuel I said hello," she murmured, her voice catching slightly. Jacob stared at her, uncomprehendingly.

"You only saw him yesterday," he replied.

"I know," she said quickly, still wiping off the board. "You're right. Never mind. Do not tell him anything. Good night, Jacob."

Jacob stood in place for a moment longer, staring after her.

Maybe there's something wrong with her, not me, he thought, hurrying away.

Ingrid

As the door to the schoolroom closed, Ingrid sunk against the blackboard, shaking her head.

What has gotten into you? She chided herself. *You're making Jacob nervous for no good reason.*

Ingrid had not realized she was staring so intently at the boy but she had been trying to think of something clever to him so he could pass it along to his older brother, Samuel.

Ingrid and Samuel were only two years apart in school but it seemed she had always had eyes for the tall but aloof boy.

When she had been offered the teaching position, she had been reluctant to take it, hoping that Samuel would eventually come around and ask to court her.

Ingrid had no way of knowing if Sam was merely shy or simply had no interest in her. Samuel Wyse had always kept to himself but sometimes, Ingrid would catch him staring at her with such longing in his eyes that the emotion was unmistakable.

Still, every time she tried to give him a signal to approach, he would retreat into himself further and hurry away.

I am pining away for a man who probably does not have any interest in me and worse, I am dragging his brother into my delusion.

Ingrid sighed at her plight and continued the task of cleaning the schoolroom before she left for the day.

It was probably for the best that she had not been courted by Sam or anyone else; teaching was a full-time commitment. She would be expected to give up her position if she ever decided to marry.

And just because Samuel Wyse does not want me, does not mean I will remain single. There are many honorable Amish men who would make fine husbands in Cashton.

In her heart, Ingrid knew she only wanted Sam Wyse but as she stared at the small, hopeful faces of her students, she was also aware she wanted children at some point in her life.

Instead of focussing my attention on Samuel, I should think about my future, Ingrid thought unhappily.

With a heavy heart, Ingrid realized that perhaps it was time to move on and forget about Samuel Wyse.

Jacob

"You seem distracted, Jacob," Mary Wyse commented over the moderate din of the supper table. Meals were always a full activity in the home. With twelve people dining on an average night, voices seemed to trip over one another.

"No," Jacob replied, eyeing his mother. "I am merely thinking."

"About what?" Eliza asked. "Emma King?"

Jacob glanced at his married oldest sister, his brown eyes amass with confusion.

"No," he answered. "Why would I be thinking about her?"

There was a slight chuckle at the table but no one responded.

Jacob turned his attention to Samuel, his second oldest sibling.

"Ingrid says hello," he informed Sam. To his surprise, his brother began to choke on his mouthful of food, coughing hysterically as their brother-in-law Daniel turned to hammer on his back.

"*Mein Gotte!*" Mary cried, rushing to tend to her son. "Are you all right, Sam?"

Sam nodded vehemently, regaining his composure and turned to Jacob. He waved his mother away.

"I am fine, *Mamm.*"

Mary backed away, taking her seat next to her husband, Samuel who had not batted an eye.

Content that order was restored at the table, Jacob returned to his meal.

"What else did she say?"

Jacob glanced up at Sam and realized his brother was addressing him.

"Who?"

Eliza began to chortle and Sam dropped his gaze, his tanned cheeks flushing pink.

"No one. Nothing," he murmured.

"He's asking about your teacher, Jacob," Eliza grunted. "Is it not obvious he's been in love with Ingrid Smith since he could speak."

"I have not!" Sam denied hotly and Jacob stared at him curiously.

"You are in love with my teacher?" he asked, blinking in surprise.

"This is hardly a conversation for the supper table," Samuel senior snapped. "Eat your meal more quietly."

The children fell silent but a round of furtive glances passed between them and Jacob tried to understand what he was seeing.

Could it be that Sam wants to marry Ingrid?

He was only twelve. He did not know much about the ways of adult relationships but if Sam cared for Ingrid, why did his brother not pursue it?

He decided to ask his brother when they were alone later that night, preparing for bed.

They trudged to the outhouse in the freezing cold and Jacob waited outside while Sam was inside.

"Sam, is what Eliza said true? Do you love Ingrid?" Jacob asked, shifting his weight from one foot to another.

"Don't be ridiculous, Jacob."

The answer was quick and fiery but Jacob did not believe his brother.

Why would he lie if he does love her?

It did not make sense to his young mind that someone would deny an affection for another person.

Jacob could only conclude that Sam did not care for his teacher and that Eliza was merely teasing the brother son when she had said so at the dinner table.

It is none of my business anyway, he reasoned. *Love and marriage is nothing I need to concern myself with for many years.*

Sam

Sam did not meet Jacob's eye again for the rest of the night. He was worried that the younger boy would clearly see the lie in his face.

What Eliza had said about his feelings for Ingrid were true. Sam could not recall a time when he had not closed his eyes and envisioned Ingrid Smith's pale face and honey blonde hair in his mind.

She had captured his heart from childhood and sometimes, Sam thought that perhaps she could love him too but it seemed so far fetched.

He was so much plainer than her, so boring in comparison to the other men in their district. Ingrid could have her pick of any eligible bachelor.

Sam, on the other hand, was shy and meek. No woman would want a man like him, he was certain.

He would never admit it to anyone but when Ingrid had agreed to taking the teaching position after being baptized, Sam had been insurmountably relieved.

Loving her from a distance had become a part of his life for as long as he could remember. Sam was not sure what he would do if Ingrid had decided to marry. He would not have been able to bear the thought of seeing her with another, knowing how he felt.

"You need to tell her how you feel!" Eliza had told him when she learned of his feelings.

"She deserves someone better suited to her," he had argued and Eliza had sighed deeply.

"You do not know how good you are, Samuel. Any woman would be blessed to have you as their husband."

As good as the words made him feel, Sam knew it was his sister's duty to say such things.

The years passed and Sam saw Ingrid often, trying to ignore the sparks which seemed to emanate from his heart when she smiled, feeling her slip further and further away.

And yet she told Jacob to tell me hello today. What can that mean? He wondered. He lay in bed, staring at the ceiling, imagining Ingrid with a warm smile on her rosebud mouth saying "hello, Sam."

It the last thought he had before he fell into a lovely dream about the beautiful blonde teacher.

Jacob

Emma was chattering brightly as the sun shone down upon them on their morning walk to school. The rays seemed to promise a slight melt of the storm they had just endured but Jacob did not seem to notice anything in this midst.

"What do you think, Jacob?" Emma asked, interrupting his thoughts. He gave her a sidelong look. He had not heard a word she spoke.

"About what?" he asked and Emma sighed in mock exasperation.

"About Christmas! It's just two weeks away. Have you prepared all the gifts for your family?"

Jacob shook his head.

"I still must make something for Alma and Sam. They are always the most difficult."

"Sam is so quiet. It must be hard to know what he likes but I imagine Alma would like a book. She is such a voracious reader."

Jacob again looked at his companion strangely.

Since when does she know so much about what my siblings enjoy? He wondered.

"Your mind seems elsewhere," Emma commented. "Are you feeling unwell?"

Jacob was not sure how to answer her inquiry.

The events from the previous day had been rolling through his mind.

Is that why Ingrid was looking at me yesterday? Is that why she has been paying such close attention to me? Does she care for Sam also?

Jacob admitted to himself that he liked the idea of Ingrid and Sam together. They were, after all, two of the most cherished people in his life.

But it doesn't matter if Sam doesn't love Ingrid.

"Jacob?" Emma called in a singsong voice. "Is your head in the clouds?"

"I am trying to make sense of something," he growled. "Leave me be."

"Make sense of what?" Emma pressed. "Let me help you."

Jacob studied his childhood friend and shrugged. It could not hurt to get her point of view. She was a girl, after all. She might understand the ways of women better than him.

"I believe that Ingrid is interested in my brother Sam but – "

"Oh, I knew it!" Emma squealed. "How romantic!"

Jacob glared at her and Emma immediately buttoned her lips, recognizing he was annoyed by the interruption.

"Continue," she said quickly.

"But Sam says he does not care for her."

Emma stopped walking and stared at him.

"Of course he would say that," she scoffed. "He is painfully shy. He would never admit his feelings to anyone. It means he would have to act on them."

Jacob had not considered such a thing.

"You believe that he likes her and is just hiding it?"

"Anyone who sees the way they look at one another would know," Emma laughed.

"I can't tell," Jacob countered and Emma grimaced.

"Anyone but a Wyse, I suppose," she muttered but Jacob's mind was already racing.

"If he is simply too shy to court her, how will they ever get together?" he asked aloud. Emma smiled and began skipping down the path toward the schoolhouse.

"I suppose we will have to help them," she called back.

Jacob stared after her, a small smile forming on his lips.

He suddenly knew what he was getting Sam for Christmas.

Ingrid

The snow had started falling again and while most of Cashton had huddled in the warmth of their houses, preparing for Christmas festivities, Ingrid found herself walking through the snowy streets.

Soft white bulbs were draped through window displays, the town alight in wreaths, candles and red ribbons.

The warmth of the holiday was alive in the frozen Wisconsin roads but Ingrid was having a difficult time embracing the glory of the season.

She had stopped in town only for a few supplies for the schoolhouse but when she left the general store, she suddenly did not want to return home immediately and found herself walking further away from the district.

Despite the impending storm, Ingrid found the crisp cold of the air refreshing and she inhaled deeply, closing her eyes to feel the flakes on her cheeks.

She did not know from where the melancholy had stemmed but she suspected it had come with the realization that she would never capture Sam's heart.

It was a heavy revelation and difficult to accept after years of holding out hope but Ingrid knew she must move on before she was a spinster, regretting watching her life slip by as she watched helplessly from the sidelines.

It was not Gotte's will for Sam and me to be together, she thought rationally but it did not stop her heart from hurting.

"Oh!"

Lost in her thoughts, Ingrid had not been paying attention to where she walked. She collided with someone with a bump and they looked at one another quickly and apologetically.

"Ingrid!"

"Oh! Amos, pardon me," Ingrid breathed, stepping back. Amos Miller owned farm two miles from the schoolhouse.

"Are you walking alone, Ingrid?" Amos asked, looking about for a companion but Ingrid nodded.

"Yes," she replied. "I am."

Amos shook his head.

"The storm is about to turn worse. Come, I'll drive you home," he said gruffly, gesturing to where his wagon sat across the street.

She started to refuse but changed her mind as she realized it was growing dark.

"*Danke*," she replied, turning to follow his lead across the street. Amos helped her onto the cart and joined her on the bench.

"Are you ready to celebrate Christmas, Ingrid?" Amos asked politely after a moment of silence and she nodded quickly.

"Yes," she said. "I believe so. I have been trying to do little by little every night after lessons."

"You are well liked with the children I'm told," Amos commented and Ingrid smiled.

"It is a pleasure to work with them," she replied. He didn't respond, casting her a look out of the corner of his hazel eye and Ingrid felt a fission of nervousness.

"I am blessed to have been elected teacher of the district," she continued and she could hear that she was babbling but she could? read the expression in Amos' eye.

Amos had not made a secret of the fact that he desired to court her but she had always kept him at bay, knowing her heart belonged to Samuel.

"The children are blessed to have you," he replied and the words filled Ingrid with a slow blush. His tone was unmistakable.

Perhaps it was time to reconsider Amos as a suitor.

He was a decent man, hard working and civil. Maybe she was not attracted to him but that could change if she opened her heart to him.

I should not waste my time pining for Sam anymore, she decided firmly.

As they neared the road to her family's farm, Ingrid felt her heart begin to pound slightly.

"*Danke* again for the ride," Ingrid told him, raising her metallic blue eyes toward him. "I will – "

"Ingrid, I have asked to court you several times over the years and you have always refused," Amos blurted suddenly as if he had been holding in the words their entire trip from town. Ingrid's mouth dropped open, surprised by the impulsive statement but Amos was not finished.

"I thought perhaps you were not interested in marriage but I never truly knew for certain and I have never asked you."

Ingrid's pulse began to race as she prepared for the question.

She realized that Amos felt the same way about her as she did about Samuel.

It is unfair to leave him guessing.

"I am interested in marriage," she replied quietly. Amos' face lit up happily.

"Would you be interested in joining me for an outing one day?" he asked and Ingrid started to refuse but she stopped herself.

Why should I say no? She asked herself. *I do not wish to spend another Christmas without someone to care for. Gotte knows it will not be Sam.*

Slowly, Ingrid nodded, ignoring the heaviness in her chest as she agreed.

"Yes," she breathed, lowering her eyes so he would not see the hesitation in her eyes. "I would enjoy that."

The beam on Amos' face lit the entire wagon and Ingrid forced the feeling of regret from her body.

I owe myself a chance of happiness, she thought, bidding Amos good night as she slipped from the wagon.

She wondered then why did not feel happy in the slightest.

Jacob

Jacob was worried.

He and Emma had developed a plan to bring Sam and Ingrid together but he had noticed that his teacher appeared to be spending much time with Amos Miller.

"What do you think it means?" he whispered to Emma one day after school when the farmer appeared at the schoolhouse. He had been there every afternoon that week.

Emma's brow furrowed in concern.

"I wonder if Ingrid has begun a courtship with him," the girl said, her blue eyes watching the pair with suspicion.

"She can't!" Jacob said, worriedly. "She is in love with Sam!"

"Maybe she's not after all," Emma replied. They stared at one another, unsure of what to do.

"Sam will be devastated if he learns about this," Jacob breathed. "How can we get him to confess he truly wants to be with her if she is with Amos Miller?"

"Come on," Emma urged, grabbing his hand.

"Where are we going?" Jacob demanded but Emma hurried him along without responding. She slipped around back of Amos' wagon and pulled herself into the cart.

"Emma! We can't steal away back here!"

"Do you want to find out what is going on with Ingrid and Amos or would you rather let your brother wither away with a broken heart?"

Jacob stared at her, unsure of what to do but the door to the school opened and Jacob knew his time for thinking was over.

He jumped in after Emma and they waited quietly as their teacher and the farmer approached the wagon.

"I have driven you home several times, Ingrid but you have yet to invite me inside to visit," Amos said. "I was hoping today I could come inside your home."

There was a slight pause and the children glanced at one another.

"Soon," Ingrid murmured, reluctantly and Jacob looked at Emma excitedly.

Perhaps they were not dating after all. If Ingrid had not allowed him to spend time with her family...

The couple stepped onto the bench and while the duo slid off the back of the buggy discretely.

Jacob and Emma ducked behind a tree, watching the wagon disappear and turned to each other.

"There is still hope for Sam!" Emma called gleefully. "We must get him to intervene before it is too late."

Together, they rushed off toward the Wyse home to warn Sam that he was about to lose the love of his life.

Sam

"Slow down!" Sam insisted, trying to make sense of the words pouring from Jacob's mouth. "You are not making any sense."

Jacob paused and took a deep breath.

"Ingrid," he sighed. "You are going to miss your opportunity with Ingrid if you do not act quickly!"

Sam's dark eyes grew small, staring at his brother.

"What in *Gotte's* name are you talking about, Jacob?" he asked, exhaling. Emma scowled at her companion and turned to Sam.

"Ingrid is dating Amos Miller, Sam. You must tell her how you feel about her before it is too late!" Emma told the older Wyse. Sam was at a loss for words as he studied the two.

"What are you talking about?" he asked, his heart sinking into his toes.

"She is seeing Amos Miller!" Jacob repeated. "And dating can lead to engagement and engagement can lead to marriage!"

A combination of sorrow and ire sparked through Sam.

"How – what do you know about any of this?" he asked angrily. "You are children who have no business interfering with adult business."

The children seemed taken aback by his tone.

"We know you are being foolish by not telling her how you feel!" Emma insisted. "You cannot - "

"*You* cannot come in here and speak to me like this!" Sam snapped. "Now off with you. I have work to do. I haven't time for petty gossip with children."

Jacob and Emma's faces reflected hurt as they stared at him open-mouthed but Sam waved his hand to dismiss them from the barn.

"Go now!" he barked and they turned, dejectedly.

As they left, Sam fell against the stall door as if his legs could not carry the weight of his body.

She has found someone else, he thought, a woeful sadness gripping his soul. *It has finally happened. My worst nightmare.*

He thought about what his brother and friend had suggested.

Should I tell her how I feel about her now? He wondered but he pushed the idea clear from his mind.

It was too late. Ingrid had found someone else.

Jacob

He sat against the coatroom wall, listening attentively for voices. When he heard nothing, he peered his head around and gasped.

Ingrid stood sternly, her arms folded over her chest.

"What is the meaning of this, Jacob?" Ingrid asked. "You and Emma have been sneaking about, spying on me for days. Why?"

Embarrassed, he looked away but Ingrid did not move from her spot in the doorway.

"Well?"

"I – are you dating Amos Miller?" he blurted out. Ingrid's fair face turned pink but her mouth became a fine line of annoyance.

"That is a very inappropriate question, Jacob," she scolded. "You should know better than to ask such a thing."

"But Ingrid..." He trailed off.

It is not my place to tell her how Sam feels about her but if I do not, who will?

Still, Jacob knew it would be disloyal to disclose his brother's inner heart.

"But what, Jacob?" she demanded, waiting for an explanation. "You should not be sneaking about like this. I don't appreciate the intrusion on my privacy. I do not wish to inform your parents but if you continue..."

Jacob's head jerked up in shock. If she did that, Sam would learn what he had been doing and it would ruin everything.

"No!" he begged. "Please don't tell them."

"Then I expect your word that you will stop skulking about like a mouse," Ingrid said with finality and Jacob nodded eagerly.

"I will stop," he promised. Ingrid continued to stare at him as if deciding whether he spoke the truth.

"All right, Jacob," she relented. "I do not wish to see you here after school hours again."

Relieved, Jacob nodded and hurried toward the entrance.

"I promise."

But as he left the school grounds, he felt a deep sense of disappointment.

He was no closer to bringing Sam and Ingrid together than he had been a week ago.

Christmas was only a week away and he still had no present for his brother.

<u>Ingrid</u>

"*Danke* for the ride home," Ingrid smiled. Amos nodded and lowered his gaze, prepared to drive off.

Ingrid took a deep breath. She had decided that it was time to allow Amos into her life.

I am going to lose a perfectly good man for no good reason.

"Would you like to – "Before she could finish her thought, Emma King appeared at the end of the road. She arched her eyebrow, watching the girl approach quickly.

"Emma? What are you doing here?" Ingrid asked.

The child hurried toward them.

"Ingrid, I must speak with you alone," Emma announced. "Forgive the intrusion but it will not wait."

Apologetically, Ingrid looked at Amos.

"I am sorry, Amos. Will I see you tomorrow?"

The man nodded, the disappointment on his face clear but he did not argue as she disembarked and faced her young student.

"Good night, Ingrid. Emma," Amos sighed.

They watched as Amos rode away and Ingrid turned to Emma questioningly.

"What is the matter?"

"Samuel Wyse is in love with you," Emma announced and Ingrid felt an explosion in her heart at the words. She tried to maintain a stoic expression on her face but she was sure that Emma could read her pain easily.

"He is not, Emma. And this is not something which concerns you," she said quietly but the child would not leave the subject.

"He loves you and I believe you love him too," Emma insisted. "How can you overlook that?"

Ingrid shook her head, loathing that she was having the discussion with the thirteen-year-old but it was clear Emma would not easily give up.

"Emma, Sam has numerous opportunities to tell me such a thing if it was so but I fear it is not meant to be."

"Ingrid, you must know that the Wyse's are not known for their outspokenness," Emma pleaded. "Sam has cared for you since you were children. Everyone in the district knows it. You cannot let his shyness ruin the feelings you have for one another."

Ingrid swallowed the lump in her throat.

But what of Amos? I have practically committed myself to him...

Ingrid knew that she could never feel the way she did about Amos as she did for Sam.

It is not fair for me to involve myself with Amos if I can't show him one hundred percent devotion but I cannot wait for Sam forever.

Ingrid shook her head, confusion overwhelming her.

"Ingrid, you must tell Sam how you feel," Emma urged but Ingrid was not so certain.

"It is not so simple, Emma. And I cannot discuss this with you anymore. Please, go home, Emma."

The look of disappointment on Emma's innocent face pierced Ingrid's heart. Emma turned to leave, dejected but not before she paused to speak one last time.

"You are our teacher," the girl whispered. "If you do not lead us properly, there is no hope for any of us."

Ingrid watched her leave, tears burning her eyes.

Jacob

Christmas service had finished and the district mingled about, discussing their plans for the following day.

Jacob hung about in the shadows, unwilling to participate in the joyousness of the occasion. He did not much feel in the spirit despite the cheer of his neighbors and friends.

At the far end of the Lewis barn, he saw his teacher and Amos Miller deep in conversation. Jacob stifled a sigh, unwilling to watch the budding romance.

I did not try hard enough for Samuel, he thought, sighing. As he thought it, he saw his older brother making his way through the crowd, almost pushing people aside and Jacob's eyes widened as he realized where Sam was headed.

Jacob stepped forward, sensing something important was about to happen.

"Excuse me," Sam mumbled as he approached. Ingrid and Amos looked up at him in surprise. Jacob's heart began to race as he stole closer to listen.

"I – I – I – "Sam began to stutter and Jacob's eyes widened in sympathy.

Oh no! Don't falter now, Sam! He called out to his brother silently. He could see it had taken every fiber of Sam's being to simply approach the couple.

Slowly, Sam turned to look at Jacob as if hearing his silent words and their eyes met, the younger boy nodding in encouragement.

"I need to speak with you, Ingrid," Sam rushed on and Jacob exhaled in relief. Ingrid looked at Amos and back at Sam nervously.

"It is not a good moment, Sam," she replied hesitatingly. "If you would give me – "

"No, I'm sorry. I shouldn't have interrupted," Sam whispered turning away quickly but it was Amos who stopped him.

"No, Sam, you must speak your piece," Amos announced. "You have held back for far too long."

Sam eyed the man dubiously but Amos smiled kindly.

"Ingrid was just telling me that she could not foresee a future with us. I suspect that she has always loved you, Sam. I, like so many others, hoped one day she would overcome her feelings for you but I do not think that is likely to happen."

Excitement pumped through Jacob's veins as Amos' words met his ears.

Uncertainly, Sam looked at Ingrid who nodded, a small smile touching her lips.

"Is that true?" he whispered and Ingrid bobbed her head.

"Yes," she confessed. She looked at him with bright blue-grey eyes.

"It's always been you, Sam."

The sentence filled everyone's hearts with happiness and Sam stepped closer to the teacher, reaching out to touch her hands.

"I have been consumed with my own bashfulness," he revealed. "It was Jacob who showed me how close I have come to never knowing you the way I have always dreamed."

Ingrid glanced at the younger brother and grinned slightly.

"I believe he and Emma King have worked very hard to get us together," she agreed. Jacob smiled shyly and dropped his eyes.

"I did not know what to get you for Christmas," he mumbled and everyone laughed.

Ingrid pulled away from Sam and turned to the boy.

"I hope you do not make the same mistake your brother made," she whispered and Jacob looked at her in confusion.

"What do you mean?"

Ingrid pointed at Emma who stood off to the side, also watching the scene with a smile on her face.

"Why do you think Emma helped you with this little ploy of yours?"

Jacob shrugged, uncomprehendingly.

"I do not understand," he replied but suddenly as Emma's eyes met his, he did. Her face was filled with adoration and Jacob wondered how he had missed it before.

Emma likes me!

A hot flush colored his own cheeks as small memories came flooding back to him, things he had dismissed without a thought at the time but suddenly made perfect sense.

Emma is always late for school because she is taking special care with her appearance. She knows so much about my family because she has taken the time to learn about them. She has hinted so many times that she cares about me and I have been blind to it.

"I promise not to make the same mistake when the time comes," he agreed. "It is time the Wyse family lived up to their name."

Ingrid laughed and touched his cheek affectionately.

"I think you are well on your way," she replied softly.

She turned back to Sam and the two smiled at one another openly it seemed for the first time in their lives.

EMMA'S QUIET AMISH TOWN

GILLIAN BROWN

145

Chapter 1

Emma stood on the front porch, looking out into the bleak distance. Her quiet Amish town had strict rules by which each member had to abide, and Emma was doing her best to be patient, but her frustration was mounting. It had been days now. *Where was he?*

Three days ago, Emma had sent an urgent letter to the Bishop, asking that he approve medical treatment at the English hospital nearby for her father who was worsening with each passing hour. She hadn't heard a word back. Yet, with each passing day her father's face grew more sallow and his spirit seemed to fade.

The once-vibrant farmer had been reduced to a mere shadow of his former self and Emma feared that he was dying.

When her Amish boyfriend Steve, had made the decision to leave her, things had reached a boiling point. Steve had been her father's right hand on the farm and all the work now fell to her father.

"I just don't think this is the will of Heavenly Father," Steve had said to her, holding back tears as he clutched a duffle bag in his hand. "So, are you leaving the Amish or are you just leaving me?" Emma had fired back. Steve had balled his hands into tight fists. "There's more to life than this, Emma!" Steve had screamed at her. His rage was a stark contrast to his usually calm demeanor. Steve had always wanted more than she was willing to give. He'd wanted her to be his wife, but before that, he'd wanted her to make love to him, and Emma had refused.

"What's wrong with you? All the Amish girls do it." Steve had pleaded, after calling her a prude. "It doesn't feel right," Emma had said softly. "Why doesn't it feel right?" Steve had demanded. "Because I don't love you," Emma said in a whisper.

After that, Steve had been determined to make her miserable. First, he tried to spread rumors with the men that she was pregnant by an English man. When that didn't work, he'd tried to ruin her father's reputation.

When Emma's father had learned what Steve had done, he politely asked him to leave. Steve had called him and old man, and had spat on his face, but had ultimately left their small Amish town, with hopes of finding an Amish wife in a nearby settlement to the South.

Unfortunately, with Steve gone the farm work had piled up.

Emma had gone out into the fields with her dad, trying to help with the harvest every day, but she was slow and had little understanding of how to run the equipment. Her father's old body looked so feeble and frail, as he struggled to heft bales of hay. Eventually, he'd slipped off the back of an old gray wagon and had cut his leg on the way down.

The leg was slow to heal, and even though Emma had applied endless salves and home remedies, nothing would make the wound close. "Oh, I'm fine," her father had said. Yet, Emma could tell that he was far from alright.

Then, two days ago, her father had pressed his fist to his chest, clutching his heart while he shook, red-faced and flustered with pain. Seemingly in slow motion, he'd slumped over into the living room chair with a low howl as she rushed to his side. "Papa!" Emma had screamed, yet he'd only stared off into the distance as thick pools of saliva collecting in the corners of his mouth. Her father was gasping for air, frozen in pain, as Emma patted his back and tried to get him to answer her as his eyes darted from side to side.

As if that wasn't enough, Emma knew the situation was serious when her dear father had begun to converse with what seemed to be the ghost of his long-dead wife. His sunken eyes glared off into nothingness as he muttered, "Oh Anne, you look so lovely, darling. I love you so much. Hold my hand, beautiful girl. Promise you'll never leave my side." He spoke to his dead wife and to no one else, no matter how hard Emma and the others tried to get his attention.

After that, a rumor had started to swirl that that he'd been taken by an evil spirit. People had begun to talk—to say that her father had been a selfish man, which hadn't been true. There were countless times that he'd lent money to neighbors and had given away his crops for free. Yet, the Amish were often superstitious people and when so much tragedy struck a single household they sometimes blamed the members of the family.

Emma needed the Bishop to both dispel that rumor and to approve her father's treatment at a nearby English hospital. Many Amish within their community had come to visit, bearing all kinds of natural remedies, bringing baked goods, pungent salves, and endless prayers, yet nothing improved his condition.

Panicked, on the day he'd collapsed, Emma had dashed from their small farmhouse over into her neighbor's wide yard, screaming for help. The entire Johnson family had rushed over, at first fearing a farming accident. Later, the young women had kept watch with her every evening since then.

They slept dutifully in shifts, hovering over dad—turning him to avoid bed sores, spooning small amounts of water into his mouth, changing his soiled linens, and swapping out the bandage on his injured leg, which seemed to grow worse with each passing day. All the while, her father never even acknowledged their presence. He simply muttered to his darling deceased wife and stared off into the distance. However, most of the time he slept.

"What do you suppose is keeping the Bishop so long?" Emma asked her friend Ruth. Ruth shook her head. "I heard a rumor that he was all the way in Lancaster County visiting a dying widow when your papa fell sick. My cousin said that when our good Bishop got word of your father's illness he made haste in this direction, but it's a long journey by horse-drawn carriage, Emma. Plus, the weather hasn't been very good. I'm sure he's well on his way though, dear friend. Try not to worry; he'll know what to do."

Yet, all Emma could do was worry. There was so much at stake.

Emma sat down, tucking her hands into her apron. The wind tousled her blonde hair as she sighed deeply. "On days like today I wish I'd just joined the English and left this horrible place behind."

Ruth shot her friend an icy look, which then softened as she rubbed her friend's back, understanding that the stress of recent events was finally taking its toll on her. "I suppose it's the hardest to follow this path when things are difficult, but Heavenly Father promises us rewards beyond measure, Emma. Don't let the stress of the situation take you down with it. Everything will be okay."

Emma nodded her thanks blankly. She'd be able to calm down after her dad had seen a doctor, after the English had managed to restore him to his vibrant boisterous self, but not a moment before. The Bishop was taking far too long, and every moment that passed, things only grew worse.

When she'd been on her Rumspringa, years ago, there had a been a situation involving one of her teenage friends, which had resulted in a trip to an English hospital. The young man's name had been Noah Brown and he'd collapsed during a dance party, where he lay convulsing on the floor. "Are you okay, man?" A boy had asked, gently kicking him with a shoe.

They'd crowded around their dear friend, weak drinks in hand, not knowing what to do. Not having any adult leadership in the strange new English world, they had no way of knowing when a situation called for medical attention. It was Emma who had quickly declared that Noah needed help.

Finally, someone had run outside and asked for help. An older woman who'd been randomly passing by with her dog, used her cellphone to dial 9-1-1 and the paramedics had arrived within a matter of short minutes.

Emma had accompanied Noah to the hospital, mostly because no one else had wanted to. He'd grasped her hand while he was lying in the back on the stretcher. In that moment, for some reason he'd reminded her of her brother and her heart had opened to him. In their Amish world, she was used to seeing men in power and men in charge, but Noah was different. Even though he was strong, he also allowed himself to feel things and to be vulnerable—she admired that about him.

Two days later, after all the tests had been run on Noah, Emma had been the only one by his side when the English doctor had quietly come in and regrettably announced that Noah had a rare form of blood cancer. She'd never be able to forget the look in Noah's eyes then, as he reached for her—a complete stranger to hold him. She'd wrapped him in her arms and had held him as if they'd been friends for years instead of just a few days. "Can you stay?" He asked her. Emma had nodded silently.

So, while the rest of their friends spent their Rumspringa in clubs partying and swallowing down liquor, she'd spent hers gently holding Noah's hand during his blood tests and endless other procedures. She'd gotten to know the hospital staff, but more importantly, she'd gotten to know Noah.

Somehow hours turned into days and before she knew it, she'd spent her entire Rumspringa by his side. Noah had actually wanted to return to the Amish, so that he could join the church and be with his family. Yet, the chemotherapy treatments he needed to live were forbidden by their community. Noah knew that if he left the English world, he would surely die. He could not go back to the Amish as they had no advanced medicine.

A week before Emma was due to return to the Amish, Noah had reached out for her. "Stay with me," he'd said softly. While most people had spent their Rumspringa in a haze of partying and drinking, virtually their entire time had been spent inside the English hospital.

They'd so often curled up in his bed together and flipped through the many television channels and free magazines that the nurses provided. In between treatments, she'd sometimes push his wheelchair down into the lobby where they'd listen to a nightly pianist, wordlessly holding hands. Then, they'd head back upstairs where they'd pick a movie from the hospital's offerings, and usually fall asleep arm in arm.

They weren't supposed to sleep like that—with her curled up in his hospital bed, but usually the nurses looked the other way and pretended not to notice. After all, he was dying.

In just a few short weeks Noah had become a part of her, and even now she sometimes woke up in the dead of night, hoping to find his scraggly blonde head of curls lying beside her. Even though that was years ago, she never could quite get over Noah. Emma had secretly thought that she'd probably miss him every day for the rest of her life, and she was okay with that. Noah was amazing.

In fact, the first time that Steve had asked her to be his girlfriend and to officially start courting, she'd said no because Steve was so different from Noah. For an Amish person, Steve had some serious character deficits. Plus, they never laughed together for hours on end the way she'd done with Noah.

Emma and Noah seemed to have just fit together seamlessly, and with Steve everything felt forced and unnatural. Noah was her first love and he wouldn't be easily forgotten. Often, Emma would lay awake in her bed, wondering if he'd made it through chemotherapy, just hoping he was somehow still alive. Maybe they'd meet again in heaven. Maybe one day she'd be lucky enough to just pass him on the street—to just catch one more glimpse of him.

Chapter 2

It was Emma who had pushed Noah to stay in the strange new English world, even though she knew it meant that she'd never see him again. Yet, at least it meant he'd be alive. "I want to be where you are," Noah had said, trying to stand. He reached for her and Emma shook her head no.

"You know that we don't have powerful medicine in our community. They'll cover you in herbs and they'll pray over you, but you'll die, Noah. And you and I both know it won't be a peaceful death." She said. He'd nodded in silent understanding. "Use the English medicine to get well, find a wife for yourself. Live and be happy. Give yourself a chance." Emma said, with tears in her eyes. "What if I don't know how to be happy without you? What if I don't want a life that doesn't have you in it?" Noah said, his voice shaking.

"And what if this isn't the way things are supposed to be?" He asked. "What do you mean?" Emma had questioned him. "What if the Lord brought us together because He meant for you to be my wife all along? What if we're meant to be together?" Noah kissed the back of her hand with his soft lips. She kissed him on the forehead and then turned away. "I'm sure the Lord wants you to be alive more than he wants anything else for you, Noah," she'd said. "What if I want to be with you more than I care about anything else?" Noah asked.

Then, she gave him one last hug. They stood locked together for a long time. Noah squeezed his eyelids shut, trying to remember the feel of her, her smile, every single detail of what it was like to hold Emma in his arms, just in case he never saw her again. Her body felt so perfect in his arms. Just touching her, made him feel a deep kind of peace.

"I'll never forget you, Noah," she said as she squeezed him tight, before exiting the room. The moment she was out of sight, she could hear that Noah had started to cry...but she couldn't turn back. She had to go back to the Amish, and if he tried to follow her, he would pay the price with his life.

In this one instance, true love meant walking away. Walking away from Noah was the hardest thing she'd ever done.

When Emma had returned to her father in their small Amish community, she'd put all her efforts into life on the farm, trying to push the memory of Noah's gentle touch out of her mind. Oh, how she hoped he was still alive. Maybe, he'd somehow found a wife and was married with children by now. Hopefully, he was happy—wherever he was.

Emma looked in the direction of her father's bedroom. Besides, her dad needed her. Even if she left the Amish and tried to find him, how would she even get started? Where would she look? There were millions of people on the planet. It was unlikely she'd ever be able to find him again.

Now that her father was ill, Emma had no idea of how to run the family farm. She knew how to bake and keep the house in good condition, but had no knowledge of farming or carpentry—and so many of their small structures had fallen into a state of disrepair. It was too bad that her brother Joshua had left them too. During his Rumspringa, he'd met a girl named Lily, and had announced to both she and their father that he would not be returning to Amish life.

It had been a slow descent downhill since then.

First, their cow Bessie died. They'd found her, laying belly-up in the pasture with white foam oozing out of her nose and mouth. Then, around three-quarters of their crops had been eaten by locusts. Emma secretly wondered if the plague might come next. But why? She and her father were dutiful and hard-working. Neither of them were arrogant or cruel. Had something angered the Maker of the universe? She had no way of knowing.

Emma sat on the sofa in the front room and slowly drifted to sleep. All the events of the past few days had weighed so heavily on her. Even though her neighbors had offered tremendous love and support, she couldn't rest. She'd lay in bed and toss and turn, feeling strange about the fact that her best friend was tending to her father while she was lying in bed. Something about that felt wrong to her.

Plus, Emma worried that it could give people the wrong impression. What kind of daughter rests when her father is dying? Yet, his illness had dragged on for days, and now sleep took hold, even though she'd fought it at every turn.

Emma drifted into a heavy sleep and felt a vague awareness that someone had placed a blanket over her. She gave a weak smile out of thanks.

In her dream, she found herself standing in the middle of their small church. There was an older gentleman standing before her, knitting a sweater—which was a strange sight for her. None of the men in her community knew how to knit. "Do you need help with that?" Emma asked.

The old man looked up from his knitting and smiled at her. "Oh, I'm fine. You know, all things always work together for good." He said, quoting scripture. Emma sat down beside him. "What else can you teach me?" She asked. "Oh, I'm not your teacher," the man chuckled. "Love is your teacher."

Love is your teacher.

Chapter 3

Emma woke to someone gently shaking her shoulders. It was her best friend Ruth. The Bishop had finally arrived.

Emma peeled the blanket off, as she stood and nodded towards him. "Where is your father?" the Bishop asked, as he clutched a hat to his chest. He was wet with rainwater and was dripping small puddles onto the wood flooring.

"He's in the back bedroom," Emma answered—leading the way. The Bishop's boots clopped heavily as he made his way across the living room. He stood by her father's bedside and clasped his hand tightly to her father's fist. Then the Bishop turned to her, "your father is surely dying." He said, flatly. Emma nodded, while tears welled in her eyes. Even though she'd suspected it for some time, it was painful to hear someone else say the words out loud. It brought a strange sort of finality to her father's illness.

"If you see fit, will you please allow me to take him to the hospital though? During my Rumspringa I learned that the English world has some powerful medicine and I'd like to take him there." The Bishop's eyes looked thoughtfully down at her father's face. Then, finally he nodded. "If it will bring you peace, do as you wish." Then, the Bishop knelt softly at her father's bed and said a few prayers. Then, he quietly exited their small home, and continued on his way to visit the next family in need of his help.

"Hurry Ruthie!" Emma called. Her friend rushed into the room and they worked hard to sit her father up. No matter how they positioned him, he slumped over like a sack of potatoes, unable to hold himself up. Finally, the boys jumped in and simply lifted him out to the horse drawn carriage. Emma breathed a sigh of relief as the horses pulled him all towards the nearby emergency room. Maybe the English could help. They were her last chance.

When they arrived, Emma was shocked at the level of haste with which the orderlies responded. They placed her father on a stretcher with tremendous ease, shouting orders among themselves and rushed him off. "Go with him!" Ruth called to her from inside the coach. Emma looked back for a brief second. "Thank you, Ruth. May the good Lord keep you!" She called.

The inside of the hospital was a lot noisier than she remembered. Doctors and nurses rushed around her father and began hooking him up to an IV. "Sir? Can you hear me, sir?" A doctor asked while shining a light into her father's pupils. "How long has he been like this?" The doctor asked her. Emma wasn't sure of how to answer. The doctor clarified. "How long has your father been unresponsive?" The doctor rephrased, a little more forcefully. "Nine days," Emma answered.

The doctor's rage was almost palpable. "So, you left him in this condition for nine days before it occurred to you that he might need serious help?" He asked. Emma shook her head. "I had to wait for the Bishop, or else he'd have been excommunicated. That would break my father's heart so it wasn't an option," she said softly. "I see," the doctor said. His tone was cold.

"And I don't imagine your father's ever actually been to a real doctor. Am I correct?" Tears welled up in Emma's eyes. She'd expected that the English would help her father, not blame her for abiding by the laws within her community. She'd done things exactly as her father would have wanted.

Emma stood back, watching as they hooked her dad up to an IV on one arm and started taking blood out from the other. She felt certain that the procedure had to hurt, but her father didn't even wince. The doctor yelled more orders to people and individuals in lab coats rushed in and out of the room. A catheter was placed into her dad, and he was dressed in a diaper. She watched as her father—her strong hero, lay there like some kind of comatose infant.

A few minutes later, a nurse rushed in and handed the doctor a few papers. The doctor looked over at Emma. "He's in a coma because he has sepsis. That infection on his leg made its way to his bloodstream, and then I'd guess that the stress of that caused him to have a heart attack. If you'd have brought him to me nine days ago, I could have fixed this, but you waited so long. I have no idea if we'll be able to save him."

Her father let out a grunt, as if he'd heard the doctor's words, and then suddenly flatlined. The entire room sprung into chaos in mere seconds.

They pressed electric paddles to his heart over and over again, while epinephrine was pushed into his IV. Finally, her father's heart was beating again—yet he looked even worse than before. Now, he was intubated and he looked like some kind of corpse on a breathing machine.

"This is a very hard lesson for you." The doctor said as he exited the room. Emma reached over and squeezed her father's hand. Perhaps the doctor was right. Perhaps she should have just taken him to the hospital without waiting on the Bishop's permission. Maybe her obedience had been foolish.

Just then, a machine made a loud beeping sound again. Doctors flooded into the room for a second time. Again, they used the paddles, trying to restart his heart over and over. "Papa?" Emma whispered, when it was clear to her that all their efforts to save his life weren't working this time. "Get her out of here!" The doctor yelled. "Papa!" Emma screamed.

He was gone.

Chapter 4

Emma walked out of the hospital room in a mental fog. Everything had happened so quickly that it felt like a dream. Even worse, all the responsibility was on her shoulders now. There was no one to run the farm but her. No one to plan the funeral, but her. She would have to carry on somehow, but all of a sudden, for the first time in her life she felt totally alone. The weight of all that responsibility felt as though it could crush her.

Emma found her way out of the hospital's double doors and sat down on a bench. It was raining lightly outside, but she didn't care. She pulled off her bonnet and threw it into the street, not really knowing why and watched as a speeding car flattened it into the pavement.

Then, she began to sob into her hands, without any regard for who might be around. Her father—the man that had raised her, protected her, and provided for her, was now gone forever. She was the only one left.

Someone placed a soft hand on her shoulder. "Emma?" The voice asked. "Emma, is that you?"

Emma turned slowly, letting her eyes adjust to the light. She recognized him at once when she saw the curly mop of yellow hair and the kind eyes. "Noah?" She asked. "Yes," he answered. At once, she threw her arms around him and sobbed into his shirt for what seemed like hours. When they finally peeled their bodies apart she was so overwhelmed she thought she might faint.

She wanted to say that she'd prayed for this moment, that she'd thought of him every day for years, always wondering if he was still alive, but the words wouldn't come out of her lips. Noah stroked her hair gently. "We need to get you inside and out of this rain," Noah finally said. Even through her grief she could tell that he was healthy now. His once frail body was now muscular and tan. He even seemed taller than she remembered and he walked around easily, guiding her by the hand.

Noah led her down a long corridor into the hospital café, where he ordered her a small cup of hot chocolate. Then, he gently led her by the hand and they sat together in a booth in the back. "I'm so sorry about your father," Noah finally said.

Emma nodded, still having difficulty processing the situation. "Why are you here?" She asked after a long while. "I was visiting a friend. I did exactly what you told me to do. I stayed here and went to the cancer ward. I married one of the girls I met there." His eyes were sad when he said that part.

"What a lucky woman she is, "Emma said with a weak smile. "Was" Noah corrected her. "She died a year ago from brain cancer." He said.

"I'm sorry," Emma said. Noah shook his head. "There's no need for you to be sorry. You saved my life." He smiled at her and then reached forward to push a few fingers through her long hair. "I just got a clean bill of health this month," Noah said. "Your Amish Bishop won't take me back, but a more liberal Amish group said that I can come back. I was going to look for you as soon as I did." He said.

Somehow Noah's presence made her heart feel lighter. Even with the heaviness of just losing her father, she felt safe and protected near him. "I'm buying the Johnson's farm." Noah added.

Chapter 5

Two months later, Emma hugged Ruth goodbye as the entire Johnson family packed into their horse-drawn carriage. Noah had made good on his plans, and had bought their family farm for a fair price.

Now, they were headed south with plans of opening a cheese farm. He had joined a nearby Amish church, though one slightly more liberal than Emma's parish. Noah's new church had both understood and respected Noah's choice to seek cancer treatment, and they'd welcomed him with open arms.

With Ruth and her family gone, things were incredibly quiet on the farm. Emma had managed to set a routine for herself, rising just as the sun was starting to peak through the morning sky and toiling until dark.

A few boys from the church had come on as hired hands, and with their help, she'd managed to stay afloat. Often, when he wasn't working his own land, Noah would come over to help her out. They'd heft barrels of hay and then spend long hours on the front porch drinking lemonade, chatting about the future. It was a lot like the old days. Except of course, for the Bishop.

Ever since her father had died, the Bishop had been giving Emma a hard time. In keeping with their traditions, he felt that Emma should sign her farm over to him, yet she refused to do so. What if the Bishop then decided to kick her off her land? She'd have nowhere to go. Plus, she'd worked so hard throughout the years. The farmhouse was her home.

One day, when Emma was working in the fields with the boys and Noah, a figure appeared in the distance. He was lean and wiry and walked with a limp. Emma strode out to see who it was, with a strange feeling in the pit of her stomach. Low and behold, it was her ex-boyfriend Steve. He was holding a heavy duffel bag and looked somewhat defeated.

"Emma!" Steve called when he saw her. Her voice got caught in her throat. He looked ragged and had those same mean eyes that she never felt could be trusted.

"It's been a long time, Steve," Emma finally said politely. "I missed you so much. I went to that Amish community I told you about, but they kicked me out. I heard about your father's death and I figured you might need a hand, so I packed up and came to help." Emma looked suspiciously at his bag. She didn't want him to stay. He'd scarcely been there for five minutes, and Emma already wanted him to go.

"You got anything to eat?" Steve asked. Emma looked over at the boys and Noah. "We have a lot of work that we have to finish by sundown, but if you want, I'll fix you something to eat after that." Emma said pointedly. "You're working in the fields now?" Steve asked. "We do what we must...and anyway, I enjoy it. It's a good work-out." Emma said, skipping back over to where the men were still lifting bails.

Steve threw down his duffle bag and angrily went to join in. Emma watched as Steve and Noah's eyes met. She could tell from Noah's expression that he didn't like Steve and that Steve didn't like him either. She made quick introductions and then they continued to work in silence until the sun set. All their laughter had ended when Steve had arrived.

Later, that evening, Emma fixed dinner for Noah, Steve, and the two boys she'd hired. It was a hearty meal of fried chicken, mashed potatoes, green beans, and yeast rolls. As she set a plate in front of Noah, he winked at her and smiled. Steve caught the moment that was shared between them and scoffed.

"So tell me, Noah, how long have you known my girlfriend?" Steve asked, after everyone had started to eat. Noah looked up, confused. "You never told me you were dating anyone?" He said. "That's because I'm not dating anyone." Emma answered, without skipping a beat. "Steve broke up with me a long time ago. I haven't seen him in months." The boys chuckled and everyone at the table nodded. Steve's face was beet red.

"Well, since your father's passing I knew you'd need a hand in running the farm." Steve said snidely.

"I don't know, it seems to me like Emma's doing a mighty fine job," Noah said, smiling at her from across the table. Noah looked over at Steve's bag which was now resting on the floor.

"I can use my horse to take you to one of the Inns downtown," Noah said to Steve. "Surely you weren't expecting to stay here alone with Emma, since you aren't married—as I'm sure you realize that could endanger her reputation with the church." Steve looked so furious Emma feared he might explode.

"And since when did you become the authority on the church?" Steve asked. "You belong to that liberal Amish group, don't you?" Steve asked. Everyone at the table grew quiet. "You call hem liberal. I call them sensible," Noah said after a long while.

When dinner was over, Noah made sure that Steve left with him. He drove him downtown in his carriage and helped him with the expense of a hotel, for which Steve did not even say thank you.

As Emma cleaned up, she couldn't help but smile to herself. Only a few months ago, she'd thought she would never see Noah again and now here he was, living right next door to her, protecting her.

Chapter 6

The next morning, the Bishop showed up on her doorstep, with a loud knock. He held a document in his hand and shoved it at Emma as he pushed his way into her house. "Last night, Steve came to me and told me that you're living in sin," the Bishop snarled. "Is it true that you've had men in this home without chaperones?" The Bishop demanded. Emma swallowed.

"I have two young Amish boys that work the land for me, and sometimes my neighbor Noah is kind enough to come over and help me with the farm." The Bishop looked her up and down with a scowl.

"You are a disgrace," he finally said. "You know that it is against the rules of our church for you to be alone with strange men. We don't allow that. Lucky for you though, Steve Ingalls has agreed to marry you and save your ruined reputation."

Just then, Steve let himself into her home. Emma's eyes widened. "Steve is a member of our church in good standing and will make a suitable match for you. Otherwise, if you choose not to marry, I'm going to call an inquest and have this farm taken from you. Those are your options."

The Bishop turned and snidely let himself out of the home, just as Emma collapsed into tears.

Through her crying, she could hear Steve chuckling. "You always thought you were so much better than me, didn't you?" Steve said. "Well, look who gets to have the last laugh now?" Steve stood and grabbed her hard by the wrist. Then, he pressed her against the wall and pushed her dress to the side. Emma screamed.

Before Steve could say another word, Noah had burst through the door and had thrown Steve onto the floor.

"Don't you ever lay a hand on her!" He yelled. Steve's mouth was bloody and he looked up at them with hateful eyes. "Get out of my house and don't ever come back." Emma said softly.

Steve brushed himself off and stood up. Then, he stopped dead in his tracks. He turned around and smiled. "Emma, I'm sorry that I never got to poison you, like I did your old cow Bessie. I'd have gotten rich, if I could have gotten you out of the way."

Steve shot Emma a nasty look and Noah stepped in front of her. "You'd have to get through me first, Steve and by the looks of it, I don't think that's ever gonna happen."

Emma clasped Noah's hand in her own as she watched Steve walk down the long dirt road and drift out of sight, out of her life forever.

As soon as Steve was out of sight, again Emma collapsed into tears. She told Noah the entire story in a rush. She had to either get married or lose the farm. "Well, that's great news!" Noah smiled. Emma looked at him for a moment as though he'd gone mad. "Well, now I finally have an excuse to make you my wife." He said, leaning in and kissing her deeply.

Chapter 7

Two weeks later, Emma was smiling from ear to ear as she walked down the aisle towards Noah. After the Bishop's threats, she'd made the decision to join Noah's Amish parish and they had welcomed her with open arms. She'd never felt more beautiful as she made her way through the wooden chapel, to stand beside Noah. Her first love; her only love.

After the ceremony, they danced the night away. With banjos and fiddles in full-swing, and all the delicious food of the Amish, Emma had never felt so happy in all her life.

Later that evening, after most of the guests had departed an older Amish man slowly made his way forward and presented the new couple with a wrapped gift. When Emma pulled the wrapping off, she was surprised to find a knitted heart.

"I'm so glad to know that you both found your way home. Isn't love a wonderful teacher?" the old man muttered as he shuffled away. Emma looked at Noah with tears in her eyes as she leaned back and laughed. Love had shown them both the way.